SOUCOUYANT

SOUCOUYANT

David Chariandy

ARSENAL PULP PRESS

Vancouver

ARSENAL PULP PRESS
Suite 200, 341 Water Street
Vancouver, BC
Canada V6B 1B8
arsenalpulp.com

The publisher gratefully acknowledges the support of the Canada Council for the Arts and the British Columbia Arts Council for its publishing program, and the Government of Canada through the Book Publishing Industry Development Program and the Government of British Columbia through the Book Publishing Tax Credit Program for its publishing activities.

This is a work of fiction. Any resemblance of characters to persons either living or deceased is purely coincidental.

Cover photograph © Carlos and Jason Sanchez,
www.thesanchezbrothers.com. Title of work: Overflowing Sink
Illustrated script by Cindy Mochizuki
Author photograph by Glen Lowry
Text and cover design by Shyla Seller

Printed and bound in Canada

Library and Archives Canada Cataloguing in Publication:

Chariandy, David John, 1969–
          Soucouyant / David Chariandy.

ISBN 978-1-55152-226-5

          I. Title.

PS8605.H3685S68 2007   C813'.6   C2007-903694-5

Old skin, 'kin, 'kin,
You na know me,
You na know me …

—verse fragment from a Caribbean tale

One

SHE HAS BECOME an old woman. She looks out from the doorway of her own home but seems puzzled by the scene, the bruised evening sky and the crab scurry of leaves on the shoreline below. These are the bluffs at the lakeside edge of Scarborough. This is the season named fall.

'You should step in,' she says, reaching for the security chain but finding it already dangling freely. Her eyes only then darting up to meet mine.

I crouch to unlace my shoes, avoiding the stool that has always been untrustworthy. I hang my coat on the peg tucked invisibly beside the fuse-box. She notices these gestures and slows with thought while leading me through this shipwreck of a home. The same drafts and groaning floors, the same wildlife calendar with the moose of September 1987, now two years out of date. In the kitchen, she sets a kettle on the element and turns the stove dial while saying 'on.' Then checks again to make sure.

The gas has been disconnected. I see this immediately and know that we will wait in vain for the flame to catch or the kettle to scratch to a boil. She is silent now and her eyes are downcast and away from me. There's a cavernous rhythm that seems to emanate from the floorboards and rafters, though this is only the lake having its say in the quiet of our brooding. This could continue for a long time. With the sun going its way and the shadows thickening around us. With this old woman, my mother, so entirely unwilling to admit that she has forgotten me. With both of us free from our past.

I do this.

I stand and unbuckle my belt. I unbutton and zip down and let my pants fall to my knees. Mother doesn't laugh at me advancing with wobbly duck steps. She doesn't panic when her hand is held and guided to the skin of a dark young man.

Here. Press your fingers against the walnut-shaped lump of bone at the side of my knee. Hold them there until my knee bends and some rogue tendon bunches against that lump and against your fingers before suddenly snapping over. With a click. My body's trick.

Her smile.

'He have strange bones,' she says. 'Quarrels deep in he flesh.'

'Your son....'

'He grandmother too. You can't do nothing for bones. They like history. But you can boil zaboca leaves to remedy body ache. And planten leaves to slow bleeding. And there used to be something called scientific plant which could protect you against curses and bad magic....'

'Your son. Your youngest son. Remember, Mother?'

'Aloe on light burns. Everyone does remember that. But there was something else. Something wet and pithy they could give you when you burns was brutal. When you skin was gloving off....'

I STAY WITH MOTHER, though I haven't truly been invited to stay. On that first evening of my return, Mother walks suddenly out of the kitchen and up the stairs to her bedroom on the second floor. I hear the low grate of a deadbolt. Later, I make my way up to the other bedroom on the second floor. The bunk bed that I once shared with my brother is still made, though the sheets and pillows smell of dampness.

My bedroom window looks out over the weathered edge of the bluffs to a great lake touched by the dying light of the city. Below, some forty feet down, a few trees lean about on a shore of sand and waterlogged litter. Dancing leaves and the tumble of an empty potato chip bag. Despite the view and the fact that many consider the surrounding neighbourhood 'a *good* part of Scarborough,' our place is difficult to boast of. We are alone in a cul-de-sac once used as a dump for real-estate developers. The house is old and bracing now for the final assaults of erosion. Even in summer, all windows facing south are kept shut. Because of the railway track, scarcely ten feet away.

I'm jolted awake during the night. The house has taken on some brutal energy, and dust motes have turned the slanting moonlight from the window into solid beams. The noise peaks and only then is it clear to me that a freight train is passing. I wait for the caboose to pass and the lake sounds to pool back. I watch the wind blowing ghosts into the drapes. I dream, close to waking, of the sound of footsteps in the air above me.

IN THE MORNING, I walk in on a young woman sitting with Mother at the kitchen table and reading a book. She has hair of wild bronze, frizzy mixed-girl hair barely kept in check by an elastic, and she is wearing the white two-pocketed shirt that Mother used to make me put on for special occasions. She has apparently set food in front of my mother, cornmeal porridge with sugar and vanilla essence beaten in. A pot of tea so strong that it seems to stain the cups and corrode the spoons. Seeing me, she stands abruptly, her hand darting involuntarily to a mark on her neck. For the shortest while, she reads my face and body before dropping her hand and sitting back down.

'I'm her son,' I say.

She picks up an eating spoon to offer some of the porridge to Mother, who purses her lips but otherwise doesn't move her face. The book is now splayed cover up on the table. *The Diatonic Mode in Modern Music*, the title reads. The mark on her neck is red. A puzzle against the light brown of her skin, the sharpness of her collarbone. A birthmark most likely.

'Are you a nurse?' I ask. 'I'm just visiting. I won't get in your way.'

'How considerate of you,' she replies.

And then ignores me, though her eyes look like they're thinking far beyond her continued attempts to feed Mother. I nod and leave quietly, spending most of the morning and afternoon in my room and staying clear.

In the evening, I'm alone in the sitting room when I hear from above the sounds of a faucet squeaking open and the deepening rush of water in the bathroom tub. I hear two voices and muffled splashes, then the young woman singing and Mother joining in without hesitation or flaw. I want to hear more of this singing and to know how Mother can manage to carry any song at all in her condition. I wait for the bath noises to stop and the drain to stop sucking, but I walk upstairs and into Mother's room before it's at all safe to do so. Mother is topless and facing me, and the young woman is standing behind her, giving her a massage. Mother's eyes are closed and she is still humming, her voice grating as the young woman kneads into the flesh hidden from my sight. The glossy wrinkles on Mother's upper shoulders and neck, the portents of her body's true damage. There's an oily thickness in the air and on my tongue, and the nakedness and intimacy humiliates me somehow. I turn to leave but not before the young woman catches my discomfort and smiles wickedly.

I hear it that night. Unmistakable this time, the young woman in the attic above. The creak of her movements.

THE NEXT MORNING, I enter the kitchen just as the young woman and Mother are sitting down to breakfast. Cornmeal porridge again and more of the vicious tea, but also a mango with a thin knife laid out beside it. The lake is unusually quiet and the sun has turned the kitchen walls lemon.

'I'd like to help out with the groceries,' I say. 'I just need to know what to buy. I could cook too. I'm not such a bad cook.'

The young woman shrugs and picks up the mango and the knife, but this time Mother's stare transforms into unmistakable nervousness. I do my best to smile reassuringly, but Mother looks away and then steals glances at me while adding spoon after heaping spoon of wet brown sugar to her tea. She has created a warm and overflowing cup of syrup before she finally manages to articulate her worry.

'What are you doing here?' she asks. The woman is looking up and waiting for an answer too, the knife motionless in her hand and the juices from the mango inching down her arm.

I don't know how to answer this question. I don't even know how Mother is reading me. As a stranger who suddenly roams her home, or as her younger son who has mysteriously returned after discovering, two years earlier, just how impossible it was to be around her. I don't know if Mother has been hurt by my absence, or if she's even noticed it. I don't know what meaning there can be between us now.

'You mean you don't remember, Mother?' I try.

This works perfectly. Mother steels her eyes and tightens her mouth. She finds her old pride.

'Of course I remember,' she says, bringing her cup to her lips.

LONG AGO, SHE began to forget. It started with ordinary things. Shopping lists and recipes, bus change and savings cards, pens for jotting down those household tasks that always manage to slip away. But then Mother began to forget in far more creative ways. She began to forget names and places, goals and meanings. She began to forget the laws of language and the routes to salvation and the proper things to do with one's body. She began to excuse herself from the world we knew.

My brother and I were the first to notice. We were young children when it started and naturally alert for the smallest signs of adult weakness. When Mother wasn't looking, we'd climb up to the cupboards and eat peanut butter and corn syrup, lime pickle and molasses. Also the most perverse delicacy we could then imagine, Crisco shortening, spooning up the white sludge with our fingers and leaving greasy prints on the cupboard doors and the walls and the doorknobs. Mother couldn't understand why she never remembered to replenish her cooking goods. Why she never remembered to give the home a good all-round scrubbing. We were never caught.

Of course Mother was minding five or six other children in those early days. Her wits were already strained to the limit. Friday evenings, the children's parents would come and apologize for the days when they were forced to work overtime at their offices without proper warning. They would smile apologetically when handing Mother envelopes. But what messages were these people passing her, really? What kind of people envelop their words? This was still the earliest stage of Mother's condition and she had already learned to conceal her confusion from others and trust that in time things would become clear. She would wave the children's parents good-bye and open the envelopes carefully with a knife, sorting through the small number of fives and tens. Dirty numbers. Meaning new safety boots for her husband and belts for her boys and, of course, more endlessly dwindling cooking goods. Money was still too precious a meaning to forget.

But soon there came the times when Mother hurriedly dressed one boy in his snowmobile suit and ushered him to his parents waiting outside. Only then to remember (too late) that these parents had a girl. That girl with the haunting glass-marble eyes and the brilliant golden hair. Or brown. She would have had brown hair, Mother reminded herself. Mother would laughingly explain to the parents just how difficult it was to tell the difference between boys and girls these days. Just look at the rock stars, she would say. Nanny standup. But her jokes fell flat and Mother steadily lost her jobs. She was supposed to be minding children, after all. She was living on the edge of the bluffs, near an active railway.

Metal monsters in the night. Dirty numbers and greasy doorknobs. This was our belonging. Memory was a carpet stain that nobody would confess to. History was a television set left on all night. The car chases and gun fights sponsored by oil companies. The anthems at the end of broadcast days.

THEN A CRISIS in something called 'the economy.' Father was laid off at the factory but later rehired as a temp after two agonizing weeks. The work was erratic. The factory wouldn't need him for weeks on end, but then, faced with a last minute order to fill, it would suddenly call upon him round the clock. Father became a maniac on those days, a blur of energy bursting through the front door to bolt cold dal and rice from tupperware in the fridge. Frantic nap. Bathroom. Frantic nap. Chugging lukewarm cups of instant coffee, then back out to catch another shift, a toppled milk carton in his wake, pattering white upon the floor.

Mother's jokes continued to fall flat. One afternoon, Father took his first long chug from his coffee mug before running to the kitchen sink to retch endlessly. Waving away our concern as another belt of sickness took him. Mother had accidentally filled the sugar bowl with salt, and Father had unknowingly made himself a briny pickle of a coffee. All four of us were in the kitchen that day, three sitting quietly until Father's spasms at the sink had passed. Such an awesome sight, his big shoulders heaving up. It was my brother who finally broke the silence.

'It's April Fool's Day. Right, Mother?'

'What you say, child?'

'You know. April *Fool's* Day. When people do jokes and nobody suspects because nobody remembers what day it is anyway?'

'Yes …' said Mother, 'you's right, child. It certainly *is* that day.

Merry April Fool Day, Roger.'

'You know, girl,' said Father, finding his breath, 'thirty years, and I still don't know how to celebrate in this country.'

MY BROTHER ALWAYS knew the right thing to say. He was older than me but also surer in his talk and more sensitive to manners and gestures and tones of voice. He figured out a while ago that Mother's condition offered him a special freedom, and so instead of going to school he spent most weekdays alone in his bedroom.

'Child,' Mother might ask, 'why you ain't at school?'

'It's a PD day, Mother.'

'PD day?'

'A professional development day. When the teachers get a day off and spend their time smoking and thinking up trick questions. Don't you remember, Mother?'

'Of course I remember, child. You think you the only intelligent person in this house?'

Meanwhile, my brother screened all of the letters that appeared in our mailbox. He could tell a report card envelope merely by its density and weight. He used a flashlight or a bright bulb to spot official school seals through unopened letters, and so he intercepted and destroyed messages from guidance counsellors who were expressing their concern that my brother was skipping even the most practical courses in shop and automobile repair. Some of the letters explained in simple and patient terms that schools were now learning to respond to hands-on students 'just like yours.' One of them came with a glossy pamphlet describing a new program where students would get to work in 'relevant' settings for half of the school year. Behind the cash register in fast food restaurants, for

instance. '*Real-life business skills…. Common-sense education….*'
The pamphlet showed a rainbow of coloured faces.

But my brother wasn't interested in school. He was going to be
a poet.

I didn't know this at first because we rarely spoke. Like our father, he seemed inaccessible and slow to meet your eyes. He was
big too, and with a bruised edge to himself that you weren't ever in
a hurry to poke at and ask what's the matter. But then, one sharp
spring morning, my brother told me to make two peanut butter
sandwiches with the crusts cut off and to take two bananas from
the fruit bowl and to come with him for a while.

He carried a red toolbox which he normally kept locked underneath our bunk bed. We walked to a secret edge of the bluffs near
the back of our home, and we slid-stepped down the slope of clay,
holding onto brush and radically leaning trees and even thistles
when a fall suddenly threatened. We reached the shore and walked
east until we got to that place where a fenced sewer pipe from the
old factory blocked us from going farther. A gull was perched on
the inside lip of the pipe, its feathers puffed up and ragged and its
legs forking a trickle of water that moved like oil. We climbed over
the fence and sewer pipe, and did ten minutes of wobbly walking
along the stones and washed up trash until we got to a place where
you could squint your mind and imagine that you were elsewhere.
The wet skins of lake-smoothed stones. The bones of driftwood
bleached by the sun. The dense silence of the bluffs towering
above. And of course, the great lake with its unmarred horizon.

We sat on driftwood and ate our sandwiches immediately, taking a bite of banana with each bite of peanut butter, the way Father once showed us. After this, my brother unlocked his toolbox

and showed me what he hid from everyone else. Books. A battered Gideon Bible, perhaps stolen from a nearby car motel. A book entitled *Surviving Menopause* by one Philip G. Winkler, MD. A Finnish cookbook with the cover ripped off. A very old leather-bound book written in some strange but beautifully sinuous script. Another book that merely listed chemical compounds following some obscure principle of organization. Other strange choices too. And why not? Why shouldn't a poet know a lot and draw from all languages and meanings? My brother took his books one by one out of the box and placed them carefully on the stones. He removed a real fountain pen and a notebook with handmade paper, the sort all rough with invitation. He sat there not writing but as if he were just about to write, and he held that pose for a long time before me.

I don't remember my brother ever writing anything that day. I remember him pointing out to me the smeared toothpaste of clouds upon the sky and the guerrilla art of bird shit on the rocks. I remember him describing the oatmeal of lake scum and the constellations of trash and plastic bottles that had washed up on shore. I remember my brother fishing a packet of chewing tobacco from his coat pocket and how he found in the trash around us a juice bottle chipped at the rim but good enough. I sat there with my brother well into the arcing afternoon, chewing and spitting. I never spoke to him about Mother's condition or Father's increasing distress because we were talking about poetry that day and mindful of things far greater than our personal circumstances and fears. I remember the bite of the wind on my face and the endless steel of the waters. I remember feeling light and almost dizzy with an exultation only partly due to the tobacco. I remember watching our spit rising in the bottle, all swirling amber and leather in the sun. That stuff so precious.

BUT MOTHER STILL staggered into forgetfulness. She wandered the streets of our neighbourhood and upturned people's garbage bins, looking for 'the good things these wasteful people does throw away.' She 'borrowed' things from corner stores and people's garages, failing to recall the concept of private property. Relying on some deeply Caribbean hunch, she kicked any dog that approached her, once sending a miniature poodle spinning around its owner like a tetherball. She became easy prey for the most unimaginative of crank callers, and she'd answer and listen for long moments before calling out for us to catch the refrigerator since 'it running,' her hand cupping the wrong end of the phone for privacy. Left alone at home, she'd forget where the washroom was and would be forced to wait for agonizing hours until someone came home to show her. Later she'd see no reason why she should wait, and we began to notice that certain potted plants smelled of urine. We tried to stop her from accomplishing many household tasks like washing clothes, but we didn't always succeed. She performed experiments with bleach and vinegar on our shirts and jeans, and we ended up wearing the acid wash look in entirely the wrong year for us to be considered fashionable.

One afternoon, she left a pot of milk on the stove that soon bubbled over and filled the air with acrid smoke. Returning from school, I smelled the calamity and ran up the stairs to a scene of confusion and teary eyes with Mother running about the house trying to find and rescue a three-year-old child from the imagined fire. When she crashed into me she screamed not with relief but with outrage. How could I be a teenager already?

'Tell me, how!? *How!?*'

ALWAYS HER QUESTIONS.

'How old are you?'

'Twelve and a half.'

'How old are you?'

'Thirteen next week.'

'What's your name?'

'Mother ... I wish ... I mean, I'm scared sometimes, Mother....'

'Don't be stupid, child. I does know what your name is. I just wanting you to say it *properly*. *Caramba*, child, just say it properly for me, nuh, and stop setting up your face like some baby...!'

THE WEEK I turned fourteen, Father took us out to an all-you-can-eat buffet. He was uncharacteristically happy. He'd voted for the winning Conservative party in the past election, and he felt that he had thus contributed in some small way to the strengthening economy that the newspapers were describing. There'd surely be the chance for full-time work at the factory or somewhere else very soon. My brother was also happy. He'd attended a poetry reading in the city and some old guy in khakis had approached him and urged him to keep writing and to begin submitting his work to magazines. My brother explained to us that he wasn't ready to show his stuff to anyone just yet, but he added that he was happy to know that there were people out there. People who cared about these things. Father said a quiet grace and then ordered my sixteen-year-old brother a beer, to my amazement and secret jealousy. We then laughingly set out on what my brother called our hunting operations, with the goal of happily confirming beyond all doubt what others in the restaurant might have already suspected about the appetites of dark-skinned people. We were sitting down with plates piled high when we noticed that Mother had disappeared.

We split up and searched everywhere. We went to the ladies' washroom and called into it and asked women who looked at us suspiciously to please check the stalls. We angered a raccoon while checking the dumpsters behind the restaurant. We asked people table by table if they saw someone leave. A black woman. Excuse me, but would you by any chance have noticed a black woman? Finally the manager pushed open a door and found Mother in the staff dressing room, sitting in a corner. Her hands were clasped around her knees and her long pleated skirt fanned out neatly on the floor. Her head was down but we could see that her makeup was streaked. I waited for my brother to say something reassuring, something appropriate, but he was quiet. I waited for Father to act but he remained quiet and still, though he clenched and unclenched his thick fingers. I called to Mother, but she didn't answer.

I lowered myself beside her. I sat there reading the soap bucket stains on the floor with her for a few moments. A zag like a 'w,' an unclosed 'o.' I took her hand in mine. Mother raised her head and looked at me. It took a while, but then she smiled.

We all returned to our table and quietly ate the food now cold and gelid on our plates. We skipped the dessert bar with the voluptuous strawberry tarts we had earlier noticed. Mother sat beside me on the bus ride home, and at one point she cupped her hand on top of my own.

'I knew it,' she whispered just for me to hear. 'I knew you would never leave me.'

I STARTED TO think about Father's paralysis that night. The clenching and unclenching of his fingers. The futile grasping. There were money matters to consider since Mother couldn't mind any children now. We couldn't afford to lose this income. And what if Mother needed special treatments? What unimaginable end was she travelling toward? Weeks later, we found that the papers were right and that something called 'the economy' did indeed strengthen, but the factory still laid off dozens of full-time workers, and temporary work became even more scarce.

Dirty numbers. But perhaps Father was thinking of something else, of the relationship that he once had with his wife. It's never good to think deeply about the relationship between one's parents, that most unbelievable of relationships. But Mother was black and Father was South Asian, and though they met here, they both came from a place where there were serious misgivings between these peoples. There was something special in their relationship. Despite history and tradition, they had loved each other.

But now things were changing. I witnessed moments when Mother would pause and stutter when she tried to call her husband by name. Those dreadful moments when Mother sitting empty-eyed might suddenly look down to see Father's fingers laced in hers, some coolie-man's dark fingers laced in hers, before politely freeing herself.

'FATHER?'

He didn't answer me at first. He was sitting at the kitchen table, his ritual before anyone else woke up, morning light upon the polished darkness of his skin. He had stopped attending church a few years ago in order to free up time on the weekends to work, but he insisted on reading the Bible all the way through over and over again, straining to commit to memory whatever he could, even the ponderous genealogies. His lips were now moving silently through *The Book of Numbers.*

And these are the names of the men that shall stand with you: of the tribe of Reuben; Elizur the son of Shedeur.

Of Simeon; Shelumiel the son of Zurishaddai.

Of Judah; Nahshon the son of Amminadab.

Of Issachar; Nethaneel the son of Zuar....

'Father? Could we see a doctor?'

'We already seen a doctor, boy.'

'But what about another doctor? Maybe someone who could help her.'

'Ain't nobody who can help her. She gone far beyond the help of men, boy.'

There was a muffled voice. Mother had left the TV on again and an early morning news anchor was reporting on some distant disaster or atrocity. Was it famine? Genocide? When do we remember these things? I only remember Father turning back to *The Book of Numbers. Elizur the son of Shedeur, Shelumiel the son of Zurishaddai....* I must have moved or made a strange sound for he looked up sharply. His face softening.

'Hey, boy. Stop that now. She only forgetting. Worser thing have happen.'

BUT THIS WAS the problem. Mother wasn't simply forgetting. She might be standing near the kitchen window, looking out over the rippled granite of the waters, when a word would slip from her mind and pronounce itself upon her lips.

'Carenage,' she might say, almost surprised that she had done so. 'We was moved by the soldiers to an old village name Carenage.

Named after the Spanish ships that anchored there long ago to get careen. Clean up from barnacle, yes? Free up from they weight and make smooth again after the trip from Africa. There was an old woman who did know. A woman with long memory and the proper names of things. We was moved, but there was a boy who get sick with the cough. He woulda *dead*, but she tell us what to make. A tea of shado beni and other bush. We all laugh, laugh in relief when she spoon the stuff to he lips. He bitter face and the flutter of he hands trying to push the taste away. He first sign of fight in days....'

'Kakashat,' she said another time. 'For sugars and blood pressure and growths....'

'Zootie. You wouldn't know it unless you had wisdom. It stings when you touch it. But in a tea it could save you life when you body won't give up it water....'

Mother never deliberately explained to me her past, but I learned anyway. Of lagahoos, and douens, and other spectres of long-ago meaning.

'Soucouyant,' Mother said aloud to herself one day. 'I saw one in the morning. A morning thick with burnt light. I walking a narrow path of dirt, you see, my ankles painted cool by wet grasses....'

Her voice trailed off. She noticed me sitting beside her.

'You know what a soucouyant is, child?'

'Isn't she an evil spirit? Someone who sucks your blood at night?'

'Yes,' Mother answered after a pause, really only the shortest pause. 'Yes, child, you is absolutely correct.'

'HOW OLD ARE you?'

'Fifteen. My … my name is …'

'You telling me you name? You think a mother could forget she own child name? You think I going crazy? Answer me! You think I going crazy? Well, suppose I show you what *really* crazy? This … *this now* … is crazy…!'

OUR LAST DINNER together as a family. We still had dinner together though Mother had become less interested in eating. Father said a prayer, thanking the Lord for the strength he gives to all who suffer, the protection he gives from the spirits of darkness. Mother was fine for a while, but then she started drifting. She was using the serving spoon to poke at the obscene dish of beef and macaroni that Father had poured for us from a can when she stopped to touch the back of her head and afterward the thin scar at her chin. She traced the lacy roughness as if discovering it for the first time. A braille, it told a story.

'Chaguaramas,' she explained. 'She loss she skin at the military base in Chaguaramas. She wore a dress of fire before it go ruin her. I wore a hat of orange light, a sheet of pain, yes, on my head and neck. I turning to her, turning to help and undo it all, but I trip up. My chin busting up against something sharp. Darkness washing me all over. When I wake, I back in our home in Carenage. They call the old woman and she here now reaching up into the tall parts of the house. Reaching and stretching like she appealing to the creatures of corners and ceilings. She gathering cobwebs, you see. I remember that she put a pillow for my head, and that she tell me lie face up. I remember the numbness at the back of my head and the cobwebs falling light like a spell upon me, the blood no longer itching down my neck. And I remember the one they laid beside me like a mother. She head completely tie up in whitest gauze. She muffled sounds not quite like crying.'

Silence around the table. Father was mechanically forking food to his mouth, spooning on more and more hot sauce and cooling his tongue with short intakes of breath. My brother didn't look up either and seemed preoccupied with the task of arranging the macaroni on his plate into a series of commas without words. Only the great lake spoke its piece, its wash and roll and wash.

'HUGH JAZZ?' Mother asked us, holding the phone. 'Is you all see a *Hugh Jazz* here?'

WE EACH LEFT Mother in our own ways. Father left first and in a hurry as usual. In a fraction of a second, the foreman informed us, after the guillotine strike of a falling sheet of steel. Mother was already in the midst of a particularly bad week and couldn't seem to understand the situation or be persuaded to leave the house. My brother was eighteen at the time and so he went to identify the body. I persuaded him to take me too, dizzily watching as they slid the body into sight at the morgue. The iron waft of blood made me think of Mother's misplaced menstrual pads. I noticed the slashed flesh on Father's neck which leered out at me like a tongue. I noticed the dark skin which had lost its beauty and turned to grey wax. I noticed Father's chest which didn't sport a single hair. Would someone have shaved his body after death? Was he always so hairless? Why hadn't I ever noticed this before? I looked at Father's hands and saw for the first time a pin-prick beauty mark on the back of his wrist.

'Sir…?'

My brother was silent. He wasn't looking at the body at all.

'Yes,' I said. 'It's him. Our father.'

Later, at a hastily arranged meeting in the factory office, a group of lawyers and foremen told my brother, Mother, and me that Father was very distracted that day and was simply not paying attention. This made sense. We were all getting more and more distracted these days. Why hadn't Father recognized this? Why wasn't he more careful? My brother shook his head silently and one of the lawyers misunderstood and ensured us once more, both gently and firmly, that it was indeed the error of the deceased. We didn't argue but we also sat silently for some time, each of us lost in our thoughts. We heard someone clear a throat but we continued to sit silently, not knowing what we were supposed to accomplish here amongst these suited men and women. After this last awkward pause, two of the lawyers whispered to each other and finally one stated aloud that the company would be most *desirous* to provide a reasonable out-of-court settlement, especially in order to avoid any potential legal misunderstandings or grievances.

'We are nothing if not *desirous*,' the lawyer explained. 'Indeed, we are prepared to offer you all something indubitably substantial. Something the wife of the deceased might draw upon throughout her retirement. We're talking about stability. It's what we all want, isn't it? I'm sure that's what your father would have wanted.'

They were right, though my brother wasn't listening at this point. He seemed to be mesmerized by a streak of bird shit on the office window. Exclamation point, he murmured just loud enough for me to hear, but that was all. Mother was completely silent and unresponsive. When the time came, I touched her arm and placed the pen in her hand and pointed to the lines she needed to sign. Her signature seemed to change on each new page. Mother's creative writing. But nobody seemed to care.

MY BROTHER WENT next. He was growing more and more gloomy and introverted. He stopped speaking to Mother and me, though he assumed a new role as the working man of the family. He got a job at the Happy Chicken restaurant in a strip mall deeper in the city. He wore a disposable paper hat. He watched an employee training video that opened with an animated caveman bonking a woolly mammoth on the head with a club, the voice-over explaining that the obtaining of tasty yet convenient food had been important since the dawn of Western Civilization. My brother memorized the specials of the day exactly as they were told to him. The maximum satisfaction pack and the super-maximum satisfaction pack. Fast food language. The poetics of the sale.

He became someone else in those days. Someone fuller and more potent in people's imaginations. Late one evening when we were both waiting for a bus, he noticed a woman looking over at us with what appeared to be gradually mounting nervousness. My brother looked at me and then behind us and then back at the woman, who at first smiled nervously and then panicked and walked briskly off towards safety, her heels clicking on the pavement. Riding the bus with me a couple days later, my brother looked up from his old and barely legible edition of A Girl's Gay Garland of Verse to see a man in a suit stifling a laugh. What the hell was this guy's problem? What exactly was so funny about seeing a young man read a book? My brother carefully marked his page before approaching the man and addressing him in a deep but even voice.

'Something *funny*? *Incongruent*, motherfucker?'

Soon nobody at all was smiling at my brother. He came to be 'known' by teachers, neighbourhood watch volunteers, and police throughout 'the good neighbourhood' where we lived. Could this be the worst of all possible fates, to be known by professional knowers? My brother reacted by becoming increasingly quiet and withdrawn, his body toughening around him like a carapace. He stopped communicating to anyone, including Mother and me.

He still sat with us for supper, his final familial obligation. But there came the day when Mother leaned over to me and whispered that dreadful and inevitable question.

'Who *is* that one sitting across from us?'

My brother heard, but he didn't seem hurt. His eyes gave nothing to us as he left the table and walked upstairs to our bedroom. He spent the rest of the night packing up. Early in the morning, I heard the front door open and noticed my bedroom drapes rustling with the changing air pressure of the house. The door closed and there was more rustling of the drapes. And that was it.

I was looking out of the window at his departing figure when I sensed her behind me. I turned and saw Mother with a pink rubber shower cap on her head, her night-shirt open, her breasts partly exposed.

'What wrong?' she asked. 'It look like there something wrong in you face.'

'Nothing's wrong, Mother.'

'Don't lie to me, dear. I know when something wrong. I you mother, you know.'

THEN MY OWN leaving. I wouldn't just leave her, of course. I'd first alert all of the crucial people at the bank and the phone and cable companies. I'd arrange for monthly withdrawals from Father's insurance for necessities. I'd contact social services as well as Mother's friend, Mrs Christopher. I'd make all sorts of provisions for my departure.

'Do you understand, Mother? I'm making *provisions*.'

'*Ground* provisions? Eddoes? Cassava? Cush Cush? Yam? Since when you learn to cook, child…?'

I packed one afternoon as she kneeled at the bathtub faucet, cupping her hand under the weight of the water and then releasing. Cupping again and releasing. I stuffed the rest of my clothes into my burlap bag. I slipped downstairs to the kitchen and began stuffing slices of bread into the lint-filled pockets of my windbreaker when she caught up with me. Mother had splashed water on her dress and was now pinching the damp material away from her thighs and looking at me with childish embarrassment. She had left the tap running upstairs, and water had already begun to drip from the cracked and sagging ceiling of the sitting room. Mother watched me shoulder my bag and then smiled.

'You's getting milk?' she asked.

'You already have milk, Mother. It's in the blue carton.'

'Blue,' she said softly, as if tasting the word. 'The colour blue….'

I caught a bus heading west toward the city. I sat in coffee shops for hours, cold skins of white surfacing and clinging to the edges of my paper cups. At night, I found a hostel room which smelled of cabbage and stale piss. I slept hard, so hard, and never again paid any attention to dreams.

'You crying,' she had asked, just before I left. 'Why you crying, child of mine?'

THE CITY WAS for me a place of forgetting. I found my anonymity in a series of rent-by-the-week rooms, in under-the-counter jobs as a dishwasher and holiday flower-seller and hot-dog vendor. I met others who were fleeing their pasts, the discontents of nations and cultures, tribes and families. I roomed for a while with a kid, barely sixteen, who was born in a logging town in British Columbia but who hitched a ride here in the cargo bin of a train. It was a risky trick, his journey east, and not everyone could manage it. Not everyone could handle the cold and dark, or know that one can drink piss to stave off dehydration. And not everyone had the insight to prepare themselves for life as a world-famous rapper by carefully studying the best of the best. Grandmaster Flash and the Furious Five, Run DMC, and, most recently, Public Enemy.

'Damn straight, homeboy. Know-what-I'm-saying?'

Once, I got us a gig cleaning cutting surfaces and machinery in a poultry processing plant to the north of the city. We were bussed to a site where all of the regular labourers were brown and spoke Spanish to each other. We were told where to point the hoses of superheated chlorinated water. We weren't advised to wear gloves or masks though, and so, when my symptoms emerged, I was told with the rest of the workers not to panic and that the blisters and wheezing would soon pass.

'Homeboy's Canadian too,' my friend explained to the shift boss, cradling his wrist and nodding in my direction.

'Yeah?' said the boss, turning to me and lowering his voice. 'Better get your dumb ass to a hospital, Canadian.'

'WHAT THE HELL is wrong with you, homeboy?' asked my friend a couple days later. We were sitting on a bench in the downtown train station, looking up at the crazily high ceilings. Our hands were plastered with band-aids and leaking a thin pink fluid, and my friend was chain-smoking menthol cigarettes. To cool his throat, he explained. I expected him to be mad at me for setting us up with such a stupid job, but he was mad at me for some other strange reason.

'What's your story, homeboy? You're always visiting bookstores and reading poetry and shit. You talk all good. Man, you talk as if you're whiter than me, and my grandfather was in the bloody Asiatic Exclusion League! What's up, homeboy? What's your problem?'

'I don't know.'

'You're a fool, homeboy! A total *fool*! You should have *'nuff* ducats by now. Nigga's got to get *his*…!'

I GAVE IN TO his coaxing. I responded to job ads in papers, but never seemed to leave an impression on anyone. I landed a few interviews but always got through these poorly, responding vaguely and unsatisfactorily, no doubt, when the questions began to get a bit personal. I eventually landed a job in an all-night coffee shop on Bloor Street, not far from the financial district. A rotating staff of coloured women, a posted schedule reminding us of the benefits of 'flexible hours,' a shift manager with an MA in economics from University of Makerere, Kampala. It was better than the poultry factory, though. And there were even small perks. On slow Monday evenings, I'd invite my friend to visit and offer him one of those hot chocolates that dribbled out of a noisy machine into a large Styrofoam cup.

'That's right!' he'd say while the machine whirred. 'Straight-up *big ass* beverage, gee. *Yaaaahhh, Boooyeee…!*'

We'd find a seat and spoon the top-froth into our mouths before adding whiskey from a concealed flask. We'd drink quickly and wait for the happy war of sugar and alcohol and caffeine in our blood. Lionel Richie played about us in a continuous loop, and the downtown lights glimmered. We had arrived. We were at the heart of it all. One of my co-workers, a woman named Carla, mentioned that branches of this shop had opened in Japan and South Africa. They were even thinking of opening in Cuba. The same patented coffee-blend. 'The same damned Lionel Richie.' I was feeling the alcohol and struggling to think. We were everywhere at once? We were nowhere at all? Had we each, in our own ways, escaped?

In any case, I wandered back.

I'LL EXPLAIN IT this way. During our lives, we struggle to forget. And it's foolish to assume that forgetting is altogether a bad thing. Memory is a bruise still tender. History is a rusted pile of blades and manacles. And forgetting can sometimes be the most creative and life-sustaining thing that we can ever hope to accomplish. The problem happens when we become too good at forgetting. When somehow we *forget* to forget, and we blunder into circumstances that we consciously should have avoided. This is how we awaken to the stories buried deep within our sleeping selves or trafficked quietly through the touch of others. This is how we're shaken by vague scents or tastes. How we're stolen by an obscure word, an undertow dragging us back and down and away.

'What?' my friend asked.

I rubbed my eyes. A dark room, the smell from the garbage dumpster, a cheap digital clock showing 3:34 a.m.

'Sorry…?' I answered.

'You were mumbling something. Sookoo … sookooya…?'

'Nothing. Sorry. I must have been dreaming.'

'Try dreaming to yourself, homeboy.'

But it was simpler than that. I wanted to see her again. I wanted to see the life in her face. I longed for her as any son would for his mother, even so frightening a mother as she had become. And so, two years after leaving her, I dropped everything and returned to her a stranger.

I'VE FORGOTTEN HOW the monsters strike. Sometimes, you won't even hear the approach. Ripples will appear in vases and teacups. Chairs will buzz and glasses chime. With the fastest beasts, the passenger trains on transnational trips, you'll imagine the house itself tugging and swaying as if alone through the violence of sound. A thunderclap. A blur across the west-side window of the sitting room, and only if you already happen to be looking in that direction.

It's late into the second afternoon of my return, and Mother is napping upstairs in her room. I'm in the sitting room floating my eyes over a newspaper, some heated editorial on the Multiculturalism Act passed over a year ago. The young woman, Mother's nurse, is here too, and she's claimed the entire couch for herself. She stretches out on her side, absorbed in a book, the tangled mass of her hair like a pillow. She's been ignoring me, but when the train passes, she lifts her head to the window in time to see the buckling curtains, the gulls lifting up in panic from the shore below. Afterwards, she looks up at the ceiling where a tarnished chandelier still swings slightly. Dust falling from one of the ceiling screws in a thin ribbon.

'It's OK,' I say, smiling. 'It's an old place, but I figure we've got at least a couple of weeks before it collapses.'

She blinks irritably at this and returns to her book. I still haven't been able to draw her into a conversation. I don't even know her name. She's reading another weird title. *Electroless and Other Non-electrolytic Plating Techniques: Recent Developments.* I try not to stare, but her birthmark looks a bit like one of those symbols on a weather map.

I'm about to leave the room and fix something to eat in the kitchen when I hear it. The sound, from upstairs, of the bathroom faucet squeaking open and the deepening bang of water in the tub.

'I should check on her,' I offer.

'Excellent idea,' the young woman replies dryly and still without looking at me.

Mother sits on the edge of the tub. She's in her bathrobe and she's passing her hands through the flowing water. She reaches down and begins to stroke the glossy grey stain that funnels towards the drain. A residue impervious all these years to even the most aggressive chemical cleaners. She doesn't seem to notice the dampness growing on her sleeves. Mother's wrists, the freckles on her knuckles, the veins upon the backs of her hand. She notices me and smiles, then cups her hands once more under the solid weight of the water.

'Come,' she says.

I step nearer and she holds her hands above me, releasing the water upon my head. Water breaks upon me, pebbles rolling down my head and blossoming on my shirt. Mother does this again, and once more. My shirt now soaked, the bathroom mat changing to deep green.

'This is it,' she says.

'What, Mother?'

'This is how you grandmother blessed us. She led us to the sea. You was too scared to go under the waters, and so she cupped some over your head. You licked the salt from you lips. Such a face....'

I don't remember this. I remember a single trip to Mother's birthplace as a young child, but I don't remember the blessing at all. It's possible that it never happened and that Mother is mixing things up. But does this matter? Mother lifts some more water and washes me again. And again. It matters that I stay still for her. It matters that I stay like this for as long as Mother can recognize me and continue.

But she stops now and frowns at something just over my shoulder. She spots through the combination of bathroom mirrors a creeping scar beneath the hair on the back of her head. She gestures to touch this, but she then brings her hand to her chin, running her fingertips along the lacy script.

She looks at me. Her face a question.

'Chaguaramas,' I explain. 'There was a fire. Your chin was cut and an old woman healed you with cobwebs.'

'Cobwebs...?'

'It doesn't matter, Mother. It happened long ago. A faraway place.'

'I know,' she says. 'I remember.'

Two

THERE'S A PROPER name for Mother's condition. We learned it years ago during our visit as a family to a downtown medical specialist, a man whose full cheeks and comb-over immediately suggested to me good spirits and optimism. He personally walked us from the waiting room into his office and asked if we wanted anything like coffee or juice. Cookie, perhaps? He extended his hand not only to Mother and Father but also to me and my brother, still children at the time and used to being overlooked in serious settings. He explained that the condition was always expressed in different ways by different people, but he admitted that he was puzzled by the many unusual features of Mother's case. How early the symptoms had appeared, and how slowly and unevenly they had developed. The specialist asked questions and waited patiently for answers, and he ended the session by politely stating that, if Mother and Father refused to agree to any more tests, there was very little that he could do.

'But take these,' he said, handing us some pamphlets. 'And please call me if ever you want to talk.'

Later on the bus ride home, my father broke the silence.

'That was a nice man.'

'Yes,' said Mother. 'Very nice.'

'Polite,' said Father.

'Yes,' said Mother. 'Oh is so lovely when you find people who is doctors but so nice and polite.'

The next day, I lifted the lid of the kitchen garbage bin to see the pamphlets half-buried beneath a mound of carrot peelings. Blisters of damp orange on the paper.

THE WORD IS OLD and has been used in medical contexts for over two thousand years to describe many types of unusual or incomprehensible behaviour. Today, the word is most often connected with illnesses associated with aging, so much so that the terms 'early onset' and 'presenile' are applied when cases arise in people barely forty years old.

There's a crucial difference between the condition and its cause. The condition is the strange behaviour itself, but its cause might be due to any number of factors such as toxins or physical injuries or known illnesses or even less tangible factors such as depression and psychic trauma. Then there are storied causes, apocryphal causes. The woman from Pickering who very hesitatingly decided to try a cone of genuine cherimoya-flavoured gelato (she said 'hmmm, very exotic,' and was never again the same). The boy who hammered at his penis fifty times a day and thus irreparably busted in mind. There were more mysterious causes too. I myself remember a bright day when Mother took me to a park near the beach. I would have been four or five. I remember Mother looking up into a cloudless sky, an infinite blue. I couldn't read the expression on her face. After this, everything seemed to change.

What do you do with a person who one day empties her mind into the sky? Both Mother and Father didn't want any more scans or questionnaires. They were suspicious about the diagnostic tests which always seemed to presume meanings and circumstances which were never wholly familiar to them in the first place. They were especially suspicious about medical institutions and offices. The scissors and hooks which certainly lurked in those antiseptic spaces. The bloody and jaggedly-sewn cures. Patients' heads opened up and then roughly laced back like old washekongs.

'Like what, Mother?'

'We wasn't talking to you, child. You just finish you peas....'

So after leaving the specialist's office, we all went immediately to the neighbourhood hardware store. My father spoke with the owner about extending the small garden on our front lawn. We live in the house at the edge of the bluffs, Mother reminded him, and then reminded him again. We wanted to plant more flowers, she added. Vegetables too. And flowers. The salesclerk nodded none too enthusiastically. Father asked about the hardiness of certain perennials and the pros and cons of using railway ties for hemming in plants. Things you'd want to eat, you see.

'But flowers too,' interrupted Mother. 'Impatiens and begonia. Sweet pea and morning glory. Pansy and … shame a lady. Hibiscus … and shame a lady. Hibiscus … and … hibiscus….'

'Hibiscus is a tropical plant,' Father explained to the owner with a weak smile.

The store owner assured us that he knew what a hibiscus was, and, moreover, that his railway ties were untreated and wouldn't leach dangerous chemicals into the soil. We left buying pansies and a sweet potato vine and promised to come back soon, ignoring the giggles from a salesclerk. We returned home and Father surprised us by disappearing for an hour and returning with four rotis from his favourite place farther west in Scarborough. Mother complained about this extravagance and offered unfavourable opinions about the competence of the 'small-island' cook who ran the shop. She complained again when the rotis were dealt out, a whole one for each of us, like swaddled children for ogres. We laid into the brilliantly coloured juices and the dalpuri and achar which they had added just for us. After we feasted and were feeling tired and happy, Mother produced a deck of cards and invited us to play a game she called 'All Fours.' She seated us around the table and began dealing, then abruptly stopped and softly sucked her teeth. Laughed a bit to herself. Shook her head.

'I'll explain the rules,' offered Father.

'Yes, dear. You explain this time.'

My brother abruptly left the table and we soon heard the front door slam hard. The rest of us began to play a game with rules that never seemed clear to me. Suits and numbers … your turn now … here, let me see what you got. Mother was explaining how I should have played my cards when we both noticed the drops of water on the table. Me reaching up to brush my wet face. Father showing his teeth, but in a strange and unhappy way.

'Is just a game,' Mother whispered to me. 'Don't be silly now.'

FINE. I COULD see their point. A cause is not a condition. And a condition is not in any real way your loved one. My parents never felt satisfied with how the medical specialists were articulating Mother's new being. I too never felt satisfied after recovering the pamphlet from the trash. The stench that seemed to cling to words like *aphasia* and *agnosia* and *apraxia* …

'… *although the SWR or the Standard Word Recall test may offer preliminary indications of the condition, one must be cautious. Depression and certain post-traumatic states may produce false positives. One must especially be cautious when dealing with the uneducated and/or ethnic minorities. Often enough, an SWR test administered to these people will result in a clear positive when, strictly speaking, cognitive dementia as discussed is not truly in effect….'*

I couldn't use this. I couldn't go further. I put the pamphlet back and joined Mother in the living room, determined to see her my own way.

I GUESSED RIGHT that first evening of my return. Touch has remained important to Mother. It steadies her to an increasingly alien world and jars her to recollection when sight and sound fail to do so. Mother may not always be able to remember me. Not always. But she instantly remembers physical quirks like my trick knee. She's also able to read something on the bumps of my spine and in my hair, a texture somewhere between the soft and tight curls of her own and the spiny quills of my father's. She recognizes the odd oblong shape of my skull and that my ears stick out.

'Like teacup handles,' she says, laughing.

Smell too is a trustworthy sense. Mother recognizes the smell of a green deodorant soap on me and warns me that it causes rashes. She also quickly notices when she soils herself. She gets defensive and asks me if I have a problem, if I'm sure I don't have to make a trip upstairs, her voice getting increasingly stern with each repetition of the question. Her hearing is good, but her comprehension has suffered. Mother often forgets the meaning of the most basic words. I ask her to pass me the butter and she pretends that she cannot hear me, her eyes shifting about the table. I ask her if she can see the bird perched outside on the electric wire and she moves her head to better see the plastic bag dancing fatly over the railway tracks. But when I begin humming a song by Nina Simone, she quickly joins in.

'My name is … *Peaches!*' she cries loudly. This is the end of a song entitled 'Four Women' in which the final and most ominously described woman announces her sweet name to a frightening orchestral crescendo. Mother still gets the joke. She laughs.

'Your name isn't really Peaches,' I say a bit later.

'No, dear. It isn't.'

Sarcasm? Is she still capable of sarcasm?

'WHERE'S MY HAT?'

'On the counter, Mother.'

'Where's my hat?

'On the counter.'

'Where's my hat?'

'Mother?! I've already said it! It's on the counter!

'Where's the … *counter?*' she asks, softly.

'You're standing right beside …' I begin, my voice trailing off.

WE HAVE VERY difficult moments together too. Mother might accuse me of stealing the avocado 'pear' that was ripening in the fruit bowl when there was never one there to begin with. She's disappointed with me but apparently forgiving. She just wants me to be a little more honest about things. At other times, her accusations are edged with violence. On an afternoon of weak light, she stands in the kitchen watching me intently, looking away when I attempt to speak to her.

'Are you hungry, Mother? Can I get you something?'

She doesn't answer but moves to the cutlery drawer and pulls out a steak knife. She holds it ready, looking slightly down with that wide-gazed look which allows you to take in all surrounding action. She doesn't want to suggest that she's hoping for a fight, but she's prepared to fight if she must. Her knuckles are shiny but do not tremble, and there's suddenly so little room in this kitchen for us each to move about. If she were to act, would she understand the result? The red oil leaking from the young man's body. His widened eyes and the thick and longing noises coming from his throat. What's wrong with this man? What could he possibly want? Why can't men just try a bit harder to communicate their feelings...?

'It's me, Mother.'

'Yes. Of course. *Me*,' she says, still holding the knife. I slowly back away from her and out of the kitchen. I close my bedroom door and contemplate how it might be wedged shut at night. I wonder why the young woman is taking so long with the groceries.

When I creep downstairs an hour later, it's to a powdery white haze that's filled the entire kitchen. Mother is vigorously shaking flour out of several dishtowels. She's been baking something that's required her to sift dozens of cups of flour onto the kitchen floor. Scatter pitted olives upon this lunar surface. Add the zests of lemons and grapefruits as well as whole banana peels. She's arranged five egg yolks on a baking sheet, the only object in the kitchen that isn't lightly floured. The blender is full of eggshells, an empty tuna fish can, a dollop of mayonnaise. A recipe has slipped a few times in Mother's head. Becoming sweet, then savory. A dessert, then a main course. Cumin sands and peppermint air.

She notices me. Then smiles, holds open her dusty arms.

'Come,' she says.

EVEN MORE DIFFICULT moments. One evening just after the young woman has retreated to her room for the night, Mother and I sit in the living room listening to some 'oldies' show on the radio.

Birds do it.
Bees do it.
Even educated fleas do it....

Mother has been humming along with the music. She now stands and beckons me over.

'Dance? We can dance?'

'I don't remember, Mother.'

'Oh you remember, child. Don't be silly.'

She moves me briskly about the room. I struggle to keep up, astonished both by her energy and her memory of the moves. We're having fun together for the first time since my return. A genuine, playful type of fun. The music comes to a close and a man on the radio begins to inform us of the softness of a particular brand of facial tissues, but we're laughing already. We hug each other warmly and then Mother closes her eyes and kisses me passionately on the mouth.

'*... because you deserve a little spoiling ...*'

I jerk violently free. Mother seems shocked and perhaps even a bit hurt. She is about to say something, but then another song comes on that she recognizes. She closes her eyes and performs some waltz-like steps alone, humming softly to herself and holding her palm low to her stomach. Lower on her stomach and lower still before I flee the room, bumping into the young woman on my way out and shaking my head no.

AND HER STORIES.

Mother is sitting bundled in a blanket on the front porch, her cornmeal porridge and tea now cold. The leaves from a sugar maple make dancing patterns on her arm, and she strokes her pretty new skin before pausing, a hurt in her face. Her eyes are far and she speaks in a slow voice.

'It happen ...' she begins. 'It happen one fore-day morning when the sun just a stain on the sky. When the moon not under as yet. Me, I was a young girl running from home. Running 'pon paths so old that none could remember they origin. My ankle paint cool, cool by the wet grasses. I run and stumble into a clearing with an old mango knotting up the sky with it branch. The fallen fruit upon the ground. They skin all slick and black. The buzz of drunken insect....'

'You saw a soucouyant, Mother.'

'*Child?*' she shouts, 'Is *I* telling this story or *you?*'

'Sorry, Mother.'

She sucks her teeth loudly and cuts her eye once more at me. She composes herself by patting her hair, marveling for a moment at its texture. She looks at me again.

'Where was I...?'

'I think you were just trying to finish your breakfast.'

'Oh yes. I telling you about mangoes. You should know about

mangoes. There are forty-nine different types of mango, child. *Exactly* forty nine. Mango julie and mango rose. Mango calabash and mango starch….'

'Are you finished with your food, Mother?'

She continues to name more types of mangoes. I bring her bowl inside to the kitchen and scrape the congealed porridge into the trash, but not before discovering that Mother has sometime earlier pulled out a sack of flour from the cupboard and scattered this all over the floor. I spend fifteen minutes sweeping up the mess. When I return to the front porch, she is still naming some damn fruit.

'Mango graham and mango vere. Mango teen and mango zabicco. And mango starch and mango zabicco. And mango julie and mango zabicco….'

'Are you cold , Mother? Would you like to come in?'

'Mango rose and mango graham. Mango calabash and … mango calabash. And mango calabash and mango calabash. Mango calabash mango calabash. Mango calabash mango calabash mango calabash….'

'Can you shut up and tell me, Mother? Can you please just shut up for a moment and tell me?'

This stops her, this young man's irrational outburst. Her posture suddenly becomes regal, but her eyes again have that wide and watchful look. She picks at some crust of food on the sleeve of her blouse. She scratches her wrist and then stirs her tea needlessly. Dull china chime of her nervousness. I'm embarrassed now for raising my voice. I sit gently beside her and take her hand in mine. Her cool hand. I hear her whisper something without looking at me. I lean closer.

'Calabash … calabash … calabash….'

Please, Mother. Please.

THERE ARE THE ironies, of course. Mother can string together a litany of names and places from the distant past. She can remember the countless varieties of a fruit that doesn't even grow in this land, but she can't accomplish the most everyday of tasks. She can't dress herself or remember to turn off taps and lights. Increasingly, she can't even remember the meaning of the word 'on,' or the function of a toothbrush, or the simple fact that a waste-paper basket isn't a toilet.

'It happen …,' she tries again. 'It happen one fore-day morning when the sun just a stain on the sky. When the moon not under as yet. Me, I was a young girl running....'

'I know, Mother. It doesn't matter. You're here now.'

'You're here now…?'

'You arrived, Mother. You told me the story, remember? There were lights....'

SHE HAD TROUBLE arriving. The plane banked around the airport for almost an hour and the pilot had announced that an ice storm was hitting the city and that the ground crews were clearing the runway. An ice storm, she thought. What on earth could that be like? What fearsome beauty, falling jewels of ice? When the plane banked a last time for the approach, she looked out of the window to see the city once more. No buildings at all, only countless dazzling lights. A land of lights.

She came here as a domestic, through a scheme that offered landed status to single women from the Caribbean after a year of household work. This was in the early sixties, before the complexion of the cities and suburbs of this land looked anything like it does today. The administrators of the domestic scheme set her up in a small apartment above a building housing a butcher's shop and a Negro hair-cutting salon, hoping that she would feel at home, realizing that no other person would be willing to put her up. It was smelly and the cockroaches ran and ran when the overhead bulb was turned on, but she didn't mind. Everything seemed wonderful to her, even the scraggly trees and slushy sidewalks. The snow-accented trees.

The snow.

She awoke one morning to see it falling from the sky and covering the sidewalks and the muddy grass of her street. She walked outside without a coat, hoping to feel it touch her. Manna, she thought, disappointed at its tastelessness when it fell upon her tongue, and then suddenly conscious of the fact that she, a grown woman, was walking about the streets with her tongue curled up and out to the world. She continued to dare things. When nobody seemed around, she slipped off her shoe and carefully inched her bare foot into a coverlet of snow. No feeling at all until, slowly, a tingle and then, unexpectedly, not cold but *heat*. The magic of this place.

Every morning she took the streetcars to the home of her employers in Forest Hill. She loved these massive houses like castles and the lamplight and the pure white snow that seemed specially imported for them alone. Her employers, the Bernsteins, were a quiet but kind and reliable family. They always paid her on time, and they trusted her with the sorts of things she's never been trusted with before while working as a maid for rich folks, white and coloured, in her birthplace.

There were challenges too, though. The Bernsteins' oldest boy was seven and he had come home from school with his tie out of sorts and his jacket creased and an angry bruise on his cheekbone. It had happened before, and there had been letters and complaints with no effect. This time, as before, he didn't want to talk about it, and he sulked about the house while Adele went about her housework.

'It hard sometimes, isn't it?' Adele eventually asked.

'You're just trying to make it worse,' he replied softly but angrily. 'People are always trying to make it worse.'

She knew, of course, how ever more conspicuously different she was. People everywhere would offer cold cutting glances on streetcars and sidewalks, or wrinkle their noses and shift away, or stare openly at the oddity that she had become in this land. She did her best to ignore it or smile back when people seemed genuinely curious, but it sometimes was just too much, too heavy. Except to go to work, she rarely left her place above the butcher's shop, surviving on oatmeal and stewed prunes and milk, and dreading the time when these would run out and she would have to voyage out into the city streets to a store. Her change always placed on the counter and never in her hands.

Not far from her place, there was restaurant with a cheerful red door and a large glass window. The window displayed many desserts and often a lusciously tall lemon meringue pie. Meringue. She'd read the word before in magazines and heard it pronounced in movies and on the radio, but she'd never tasted it. A fluffy sweetness as exotic as snow. After work, each day leading farther down the darkening corridor of fall toward winter, she would pass by the restaurant window, eyeing the pie as it grew smaller and smaller with each slice sold away until a whole new pie was set in its place.

In the week leading up to the holidays, after the Bernsteins gave her her last payment for the month in advance and then left for the States to spend time with their relatives, she built up her courage and decided that she would buy a piece.

She enters to the chiming of bells on the door of the restaurant and then the shushing of sound and the dead weight of disapproval in the room. She knows that there are many people sitting in the restaurant, she knows this from looking in the window, but now she can't seem to make out details of any single person. She holds her handbag with two hands in front of her for strength, but also to show that she's a lady. There are giggles from deep in the room and around and behind her too. The men pushing back their chairs in preparation for trouble. The wooden grating of heroic men.

'Look what just walked in,' a voice says.

Nobody comes to seat her. She's not sure what to do, and so she moves toward an empty table. She sits down and still nobody comes. Finally, a man with salt-and-pepper hair and a nice white shirt slides into the seat. He asks if she wants to fuck. He asks again, and she hears but doesn't hear, and she looks around again. She becomes embarrassed by this, embarrassed for the others in the restaurant who would have to hear this language. The man leaves and another man approaches. He's the owner and he softly explains that this is a family restaurant and that no coloureds or prostitutes are allowed to eat here, though he knows of other places on another street where she would be welcome. He knows that she hasn't come to his country to cause trouble and he hopes that she will understand and respect the rules of this here place. She shakes her head yes, she shakes her head no, and then leaves through the noisily chiming door.

SHE'S BECOME TOO sensitive, she tells herself. She's living the dream of countless people in her birthplace, stuck back there with the running sores of their histories. She's been given a chance in a new land. She's one of the lucky ones. She must always remember that.

CHRISTMAS EVE arrives suddenly. She's only been here a couple of months and she has no friends or family, though she tells herself this is fine. She has none of the things that remind her of Christmas, the parang music, the punch-o-crème and rum punch too. She sees instead a blanket of snow. A white Christmas. They really exist. On Christmas Eve, she makes a lunch of sardines and a dinner of macaroni and then cleans up and decides to go to mass. She waits for the subway and boards a train before realizing that it's far too early. She travels up and down the route, sitting in the corner of the cab and not caring anymore if people stare at her. Back and forth, her chin buried in her scarf.

Union and King. And Queen and Dundas. And College and Wellesley. And Bloor and Rosedale....

'Last stop,' says someone. She nods and the train moves again.

And Eglinton and Davisville. And St. Clair and Rosedale. And Bloor and Wellesley....

'Last stop,' someone else says. Over and over again.

After some unknowable period of time, she gets off and walks the rest of the way downtown, looking for a church. She finds a small place with stained glass and an announcement in a different language. She knocks at the door but receives no answer. She continues to knock and an old olive-skinned priest finally answers, a short man with a meaty face. He chews on something and after swallowing passes the sleeve of his robe over his mouth, a waft of garlic from him. A pang of longing passes through her and she feels herself choking. Even just the scent of garlic.

'It's seven o'clock. What are you doing here?' he says. A thick accent, but one she somehow understands.

She wants to answer the question. She doesn't want to cry and she won't. The priest frowns at this pretty Negro woman battling herself and he looks around to the empty street and back into the dark church behind him. He motions her inside with a flick of his short thick neck, checking the street once more.

He leads her into the foyer and tells her to wait. She sits and stares at the stained glass and the untranslated scenes of saintly activity before she realizes that he's been gone for an unexpectedly long time. How long has she been left sitting in the dark foyer for-ever? Why is she losing her sense of time these days? She is about to leave when she notices a glow coming from deeper in the building. She walks slowly toward it, creeping along the walls and expecting something mean, some final cruel trick, as she pushes the doors open into the chapel.

Lights. Hundreds, maybe thousands of lights. There are lit candles everywhere, weeping wax tears in all of the alcoves and all of the tables. The priest is stretching up his dumpy frame and struggling with a lighter, trying to reach the last of a set of candles in an alcove. There is a woman there, a dark-skinned woman with a child. A scar on her face, the words *Matka Boska Czestochowska* written underneath and explaining something. Who is this wom-an? How did she get to be here of all places? The candles around her are just beginning to bleed and the lights are now coming from all places at once, a shimmering brilliance flooding her eyes.

'HAS SHE EVER asked you for lemon meringue pie?' I ask.

The young woman doesn't respond. She's been wrestling for almost half an hour with the gas valve behind the stove, which appears to be stripped or stuck. She curses through gritted teeth as she tries again with the wrench. I've offered to help and she's told me to mind my own business. She picks up the wrench and tries again, but it slips, and she bumps her elbow against the wall. She swears and nurses it for a moment.

'What on earth are you going on about?' she finally responds.

'Lemon meringue pie. Has she ever asked you for this? It was one of her favourite things. She used to get so excited about having it, but then she'd make the strangest face when eating. A two-ness.'

'A two-ness?'

'You know. The velvet sweet and sharpness at once. A two-ness.'

'So what look did she have when she saw you again? I mean, when you showed up here a few days ago after abandoning her for two years? Was it two-ness on her face again, or just plain disgust?'

SHE'S A COMPLICATED matter, this nurse. She delegates housework to me, mostly by leaving notes on scrap paper explaining that we are out of milk, that the hallway is getting dusty, that we both prefer full cream over milk in our tea. 'We,' meaning everyone in the household except me. Two notes on the kitchen table, one stuck to the bathroom mirror with tape, one upon my sneaker warning me to take off my shoes before entering next time. Otherwise she ignores me.

She's so casual about my presence that I start glancing at myself in mirrors around the house, especially the dusty warped one in the entrance hall. My forehead and mouth, my nose and ears. Those definitely aren't Mother's ears. Am I really so obviously her son? Is it wise for this young woman to so quickly take me at my word? I steal glances at her in turn. Her lashes and the lush dart of her eyebrows. Her thin back and her collarbones. Her birthmark a comet, maybe. A flare of energy travelling down her neck. She dresses in jeans and women's shirts mostly, though she sometimes pinches things from hangers in my room. Shirts from my childhood, a sweater and a pair of socks. She leaves books about the house. Unrelated titles like *Konansha's Romanized Japanese-English Dictionary*, and *Vocational Training in Latin America*, and *The Complete Book of Inflatable Boats*. A few of the books appear to be second-hand coursebooks with titles like *The Republic* and *Molecular Chemistry*. I pick up one entitled *On the Advantage and Disadvantage of History for Life*, and it falls open to a dog-eared page with a passage underlined in pencil:

> *... it is possible to live with almost no memories, even to live happily as the animal shows; but without forgetting it is quite impossible to live at all. Or, to say it more simply yet: there is a degree of insomnia, of rumination, of historical sense which injures every living thing and finally destroys it, be it a man, a people or a culture. ...*

'I'VE NOTICED you're reading Nietzsche,' I mention to her later.
'What?'
'Nietzsche. The philosopher. The *German* philosopher,' I add, hoping to appear knowledgeable.
She sighs at this. She hurries to the front door dressed in grey

drawstring sweatpants and an old Jimi Hendrix concert-style T-shirt. My sweatpants and my shirt. She tugs on a sports jacket and then rummages in the closet for her shoes.

'So you've studied nursing?' I try. 'You've studied old people nursing...?'

'Palliative care.'

'Yes. Palliative care. Is that your thing, your specialty?

More silence as she sits to lace on her runners, her left knee to her chin and now her right. I can't seem to help myself from talking.

'You know, it's kind of funny. But I don't think we've really introduced ourselves.'

'Cindy,' she says.

'Is that with a 'C'? Like the model, Cindy Crawford?'

'Yes. Like that.'

'What's your last name?

'Crawford.'

She stands and puts on a baseball cap, struggling a bit with her voluminous ponytail. She brushes some loose strands from her face and she turns to open the door.

'Cindy?'

'What do you want from me?'

'I know I don't deserve much. I don't deserve any answers at all, and so I won't ask for them. I just want know that Mother is safe. That she's in someone's hands.'

I've tried to say this in as unemotional a voice as possible, but there's something ragged that I can't help. The young woman doesn't look back at me but removes her cap and struggles once more to fix it satisfactorily on her head. She takes the security chain off the door and exits.

'Meera,' she says, just before pulling the door shut.

FROM THE WINDOW in Mother's room, I catch a glimpse of her jogging down the main road, back straight and hands calm and relaxed, her ponytail bobbing heavily in a regular rhythm. She disappears from sight.

'*Meera*,' I repeat aloud. 'Hello, my fitness-conscious and self-righteous name is *Meera*. Pleased to meet me.'

I have a bit of time. I move quickly to the storage room on the second floor which is cluttered with chests and boxes and bicycle parts. I locate the retractable ladder leading up into the attic, wincing at the grating noise it makes when being pulled down. For some stupid reason, I softly call out hello, *hello*, then test the ladder with my foot before slowly climbing up into the cramped space which has now become her home.

The lake sounds are always strongest up here. At the back of the attic is a porthole of smoky glass and a mattress at one end of the sloping roof. The bed is unmade and beside it is a cup of coffee with drying dregs and a bowl with a bit of sodden breakfast cereal at the bottom. Also beside the bed are some chunky looking rings, one a big glass bauble with a plastic spider suspended within. There is a whole bunch of books scattered about, again with wildly dissimilar titles, but what catches my eyes are the some half-dozen clay pieces set out about the floor of the room, rough hand-shaped bowls and plates and a smoother and more abstract form suggesting a human limb. All seem made of the same crude and unbaked material, a reddish clay with beige streaks and crumbly particles suspended within. Clay from the bluffs, perhaps.

As I reach for one, they all begin to buzz of their own strange life. I'm startled for a moment before I recognize the passing of the commuter train, the noise then fading away. I contemplate leaving the attic, but then notice an old chest of drawers in the corner. I open it and find a stash of shirts and pants, underwear and socks. I notice that two pairs of socks are my own. I retrieve these and then after a moment of hesitation pocket a pair of Meera's underwear too, which are blue and ordinary. I look once more about the attic before stepping down the ladder backwards into the storage room, humming to myself.

Meera has already returned. She is leaning with crossed arms in the doorway of the room, a V of sweat on the front of her top just above Jimi Hendrix's afro and bandanna. She is looking at something on the floor, and I follow the line of her sight to her underwear which has slipped out of my pocket during my climb down.

'Just wash them when you're finished,' she says.

'I wasn't … I mean, I'm not going….'

'I mean it. Warm water, not hot. And hang to dry.'

I PASS MOTHER in the bathroom a couple hours later. The tap isn't running, but she's sitting on the side of the tub and humming softly while running her fingernails between the wall tiles and then inspecting the material under her nails.

'Does she frighten you?' I ask her softly.

'Who, dear?'

'You know. The stranger.'

'Oh,' she laughs. 'You don't have to worry, dear. He my youngest son.'

I DECIDE THAT I won't stick around for the charade of dinner. I eat a bowl of cereal in the mid-afternoon and dress hurriedly in my room for a long walk. I head downstairs and find Mother standing near the front door with its glazed side-pane, the translated light of the setting sun upon her. She's wearing her bathrobe and she purses the robe into a collar around her neck when looking at me. I pass her as carefully as possible.

'I'm just going out, Mother.'

'Out…?'

She looks behind her now as if sensing something from the growing dark of her home. I put on my runners then change my mind. I rummage around the back of the closet and eventually slip my feet into the leathery skins of my father's old work-boots, still supple after all these years. Cold steel toe.

'I'm just going for a walk, Mother. I'll be back.'

'I … be … back,' she repeats, slowly, looking back into her home again.

I tell her 'bye' twice and step out into the driveway and into the cul-de-sac, the lights of the better houses and properties of this neighbourhood just beginning to show across the train tracks and in the distance.

FOR A LONG TIME, I never understood what ever could possess my parents to live here. This lonely cul-de-sac in the midst of 'a good neighbourhood,' this difficult place that none of our neighbours would ever have settled for. It could have been the great lake, of course. That mirage of steel and pastels stretching out to the very horizon of the world, that inland sea inspiring all sorts of reckless imaginings. My parents couldn't have been impressed by the house itself, its dilapidated and rotting frame, its peeling eggshell paint, its windows cloudy with cataracts or roughly boarded up, all blasted with the sounds of passing trains. They couldn't have been inspired by the idea of long-term ownership, since any fool could see that the lake was slowly advancing, eroding inches of the backyard each year.

I can imagine the scene they would have made during the first few weeks of renovations. Mother in her straw hat and flowered skirt, pads of foam tied around her legs for greater comfort when kneeling. She would have had to kneel occasionally even when she wasn't planting her beloved annuals, or clearing the brush around the gardens and plots grown wild, or bagging up the months of trash dumped in the cul-de-sac when the property was yet unclaimed. When she moved to this neighbourhood, she was newly pregnant with my older brother and increasingly tired. Father was his old manic self, spending long days repairing damaged walls and laying down new pipes, and wiring and repainting and insulating every room including the attic with fibreglass, though paying for this activity with a week of nights when every inch of his naked flesh seethed with fearful itchiness. He would also have been on the roof to paint and re-tile, and perhaps this is how they first met a neighbour curious enough to wander down that lonely cul-de-sac. Mother on the ground pulling off a stained and odorous glove and extending her bare hand. Father calling above from the roof, a dark angel in the sky. His greeting ordinary and apocalyptic at once.

'Morning, neighbour.'

This was the historic community of Port Junction, you see. It was considered one of the last remaining 'good' parts of Scarborough, meaning distant from the growing ethnic neighbourhoods to the west. There were no high-rises here, and the homes were almost all new and fully detached and on sensible non-eroding properties. Many properties sported antique lawn ornaments and the sort of 'rustic' fencing you can buy at hardware stores. Many postboxes bore silhouette illustrations of horses and buggies as well as family names in old-fashioned scripts. The Mackenzies, the Rosses, the Laurences. There was also a large sign farther down the main road, originally put up by a property developer but maintained by the community thereafter. The sign read 'Old Port Junction: The *Traditional* Community by the Lake.' It showed a picture of a boy on a beach bending down to pick up a shell. His mother and father were looking out upon the lake, their eyes and the waters a perfectly matching blue.

Also, there was the annual Heritage Day parade. Every year in spring, our neighbours would organize a march that would pass by the main road just beyond our cul-de-sac. The flyers explained that *everyone* was invited to participate, since the Heritage Day parade was being revamped these days to recognize 'people of multicultural backgrounds,' and 'not just Canadians.' But Father always seemed to be working, and Mother couldn't ever remember the day when the parade took place. And trouble grew in later years when she couldn't remember the parade in the first place but would peer out from behind the kitchen drapes, observing with wide eyes the spectacle passing slowly by on the main street. What was happening? Why the costumes and uniforms and semi-orderly marching? Was it serious? Was there a war or a violent expulsion underfoot? Every year, I had to explain that this was just a parade, a celebration. 'A *performance*, Mother. Just a performance.' I felt especially compelled to explain the distressingly amateurish bagpiper. His puffed lips at odds with the sounds he made. His soul-shuddering cry.

'It's an instrument, Mother.'

'Yes,' she said softly, clutching the collar of her bathrobe.

'Mother? It's a *musical* instrument, Mother. *Music.*'

'Yes. Of course. *Music.*'

Then one Heritage Day, Mother disappeared. She had been wandering more than usual, and I had promised myself to keep an eye on her, but I only remembered when the noises of Heritage began to grow. I called out and looked around the house before recognizing the severity of the situation. The noises from outside swelled and I looked despairingly out the kitchen window and down the cul-de-sac toward the passing parade. I didn't want to go outside, but I had no choice anymore. I threw on my shoes and a coat and opened the front door, prepared to run across the tracks and into that crowd of eyes and beyond to wherever my mother might be.

I saw and froze.

Mother was without a blouse or skirt or pants but mercifully in a bra and pantyhose. At the same time, she was wearing at least half a dozen pairs of underwear that she had somehow yanked up, one over the other. She was wearing shoes. Somehow, it was important for me even in that moment to check that she was wearing shoes. I realized that the parade had come to a halt. The participants were looking at Mother in their midst and also down the cul-de-sac at me. Some were leaning toward each other to whisper, and others were gesturing to get the attention of those farther away. I wanted to vanish. I wanted to get away, but then another parade seemed to start. Mother was now being helped somewhat unwillingly toward her home by an older man and woman. She seemed, magically, to grow to inhuman proportions. She swelled as big as one of those inflatable puppets you sometimes see on poles at parades. As looming and caricatured and awkwardly handled as that. Coming toward me. Coming home.

I still hadn't moved from the porch. I froze before that image and sea of faces until the two old folks helping Mother stopped in front of me.

'Brave face,' said the old woman, smiling gently. 'It's OK now. Just help your mother inside.'

'She's OK, now, lad,' said the old man, an arm missing from the sleeve of his uniform.

'My god, what's he waiting for…?' yelled a middle-aged woman in a flamboyantly blue pioneer costume.

'Have you noticed them?' said a man holding a bell and wearing a tricorne hat. 'The boys? They're *always* like that. They're always shrinking away and skulking about. They never meet your eyes….'

'… his *mother*, for god's sake. And he just *stands* there. I mean, what kind of people are we allowing to live here, anyway?'

I CAN'T FIND HER.

I've returned from my walk and searched the entire house but Mother's nowhere to be found. She isn't in the sitting room or her bedroom. The bathroom is empty. I run downstairs to check the front door closet, noticing that Mother's coat is still there, her slippers and sneakers too. A good sign, a bad sign? An old woman barefooted and lost in the dark and cold?

I race back outside and look nervously down the railway tracks. I turn and call out toward the neighbourhood, but my voice seems to fall flat and empty upon the houses in the distance. The eyes of their windows.

I'm desperate enough to run up to the storage room and shout up the ladder.

'Mother has disappeared.'

'How could she have disappeared?' shouts Meera. 'Weren't you watching her!?'

'I went out for a walk.'

'You were supposed to be watching her!'

'You never explained that!' I cry. 'You never explain anything!'

She steps quickly down the ladder, a sweater in her mouth and cursing through clenched teeth. I follow her down to the first floor of the house and watch her stamp on her sneakers before stepping outside, the laces trailing behind her.

'Adele?' she yells from the porch.

'I tried calling already....'

'I'll check the tracks and beach,' she says. 'You ask the neighbours down the road.'

'Shouldn't we both check the beach?'

'Just ask the damn neighbours!'

She yells out 'Adele' again before disappearing behind the house. I suddenly feel weakened by the whole situation. I hear Meera call 'Adele' once again, though the cry is faint now and probably from the beach itself. I step inside the house just for a moment, just to catch my strength before the search. I close the door behind me and then press my back against it before sinking to the floor right there. I close my eyes and hear the ticking of the safety chain. I then hear something else, a dull scraping sound coming from the basement. The door leading to the unfinished basement is slightly ajar.

'Mother?' I call softly from the top of the stairs.

'Wait, dear. Just a minute.'

I push the door open and catch a few dusty angles of light slanting in from the basement window. My eyes take a while to get adjusted to the weak light, but I can just make out the piles of storage chests and bins and boxes. I hear the noise once more and sharpen my eyes upon its source, and there, sitting in a corner beside an aluminum tin, is Mother. She dips her hand into the tin and removes something. She looks at what she has found and discards it and dips her hand in again. It's impossible to see what she's looking at. Even her eyes are hollow in this light.

'Mother?' I call again.

'I'm finding ...' she begins, but then trails off. The tin beside her is full of pictures and she chooses one of her husband and inspects it upside down and then right side up before discarding it to the side. When I help her to rise, I notice that she has been sitting on a damp part of the basement floor and that the seat of her pants is wet.

'I feeling cold,' she says, shyly touching the wet material.

'Lets go upstairs, Mother.'

My hope is first to lead Mother to the front door and catch sight of Meera to call off the search in some unobtrusive way. But when I open the front door, I see a car pull up with flashing lights. Someone has called the police.

The officer inside seems to be alone and he checks a few things on his dashboard console before stepping out of the car and slipping his stick into his belt.

'Hello, sir.'

'Hello.'

'Is this your mother?'

'Yes. She's … she's feeling quite a bit anxious right now....'

'Are you OK, ma'am? Hello? So how long was she missing, sir?'

'A couple hours maybe,' I say.

'Normally, you're not supposed to report missing persons until twenty-four hours have passed. Do you understand this?'

'I didn't call the police. Someone else....'

'I know. It's just for your future reference. Do you live here?'

'Yes,' I say, noticing Mother's attention upon me. 'I'm her son. I was away but I'm back now. I'm staying here for a while.'

'Anyone else living here?'

'Nobody, really.'

'Nobody, really?' he repeats pointedly, taking out a pad and pen.

'Just Mother's nurse. A woman … a woman named Cindy.'

'Cindy who?'

'Cindy Crawford.'

I notice his handwriting is extraordinarily neat.

'So what type of medical condition does your mother have, sir?'

'She's basically alright,' I begin. 'She just gets a bit anxious and confused sometimes....'

'Could you be a bit more precise, sir? We've been getting complaints and we need to keep records.'

'Records?'

'Yes. So we can know. So we can help.'

I look at Mother again. She's smiling now.

'Sir?'

'She has presenile or early-onset dementia.'

'Dementia,' he repeats as he writes.

'Dementia?' asks Mother, softly.

'It means that she's forgetting,' I explain, 'or that she's confused, or even … even that she's remembering….'

'Thank you, sir. I know what dementia is. Well, I guess that's about it for now.'

'Wait,' I say. 'I should explain….'

'Yes?'

'She … she saw a soucouyant.'

'A what?'

'Not literally,' I explain. 'At least I don't think so. I mean, it's not really about a soucouyant. It's about an accident. It's about what happened in her birthplace during World War II. It's a way of telling without really telling, you see, and so you don't really have to know what a soucouyant is. Well, I guess you do, sort of. What I mean is, I'm not an expert on any of that sort of stuff. I was born here, you see. Not exactly here, of course. In a hospital farther west. But here, as in this land.'

The officer just stares. I know that I've been babbling idiotically. I know this is completely irrelevant. He closes his pad and clicks his pen.

'Just remember to wait twenty-four hours next time.'

'Sure. OK.'

He steps back into the car and consults his console once again before backing out and driving away. Dwindling red of his taillights in the dark. I'm guiding Mother inside when she leans into me.

'Have I ever told you about you father? About how we met? About how he bicycle in this city place here?'

'Yes, Mother. You have.'

'You just wait until he get home tonight. We'll sit down all to-gether and tell you the whole story.'

S S oooucooo

~~souea~~

Three

THEY MET IN A city that doesn't exist anymore. A city that perhaps never really existed, though you'll sometimes hear people talking about it. A city where people cared for each other and children were allowed to play outside unattended. A city before the new dark-skinned troubles and the new dark-skinned excitements. A city where rice and pasta were still considered 'ethnic foods,' and one of the few places where a newcomer might have a chance of getting her hands on breadfruit or fresh coconut or the sunny heft of a mango was at the Kensington Market.

It was early one morning at the height of summer. Adele was walking through the congested lanes of the market, and she had passed vendors calling out to her from behind arrangements of plantain or dried shrimp or okra. She had glimpsed under a rude canvas tent three live chickens and a goat, their freshness unchallengeable. She felt alive in this place, attuned at once to dozens of different voices and smells, but she didn't notice him at first, the dark young man in short pants, on a bicycle and carrying a massive satchel of flyers and newspapers across his back. He peddled recklessly near, a blur of kakhi and pumping knees, a waft of something discomfortingly familiar. She wheeled to look back at the young man cycling away down the congested street, his satchel swaying with each near avoidance of crates and small children, his calf muscles black-brown and pulsing with liquid energy.

'Coolie fool!' she shouted. 'You almost run me down!'

He stopped and turned around. They didn't know each other, but there was history between them all the same. There were mildewed explanations for why they shouldn't ever get along. An African and South Asian, both born in the Caribbean and the descendants of slaves and indentured workers, they had each been raised to believe that only the other had ruined the great fortune that they should have enjoyed in the New World. They had been raised to detect, from a nervous distance, the smell that accompanied the other. Something oily that saturated their skins, something sweet-rotten and dreaded that arose from past labours and traumas and couldn't ever seem to be washed away.

'Sorry, sister,' answered the man on the bike.

'Who the hell you calling sister!?'

Adele watches now as the young man begins his dismount by swinging a leg over the seat of his still moving bicycle. He sails on one foot for a couple dozen feet before stepping off, parking, and walking to a stall in one fluid gesture. She watches him tug a paper from his satchel without looking and pass it to a vendor with an enormous brown moustache. The vendor immediately rolls the paper into a tight stick and uses it to conduct his banter. How long has it been, the vendor asks, gesturing about. What kind of *trash* is this and why isn't it ever on time? If it's *trash*, it should at least be on time. He says the word 'trash' in a pleased way, as if he has just learned the word, and the young man smiles as if the whole encounter is perfectly ordinary. He moves to another stall and then another, handing out more papers, and she sees, now, that they are in many different languages. One vendor, an old Asian woman, unsmilingly receives a paper in what looks to be Chinese characters and then carefully counts out four Scotch bonnet peppers into the man's hand, which he slips into his pocket.

Scotch bonnet peppers! How on earth, she thinks, burning with jealousy.

The man notices that she's still looking at him. He seems to think that she's admiring him. He seems, quite foolishly, to think that this could ever be the case. He finishes handing papers to vendors on this block, and steps back onto his bike, balancing smartly on two wheels as he swings his leg over. He does a tight circle in the congested street, narrowly missing a box of okras before heading back her way. A world of news in his satchel, the burnt chocolate darkness of his shins. It's been so long since she's seen anyone with such skin. Like wet earth. Like molasses.

About twenty yards in front of her and nearing fast, he lifts his finger to be sure of her attention. He lifts his hand off the handlebars and stands up on the pedals. His hands stretch outward for balance, waver for a couple of moments, then become perfectly still. He glides like this for seconds down the congested street, his eyes long-focused in concentration, past a dozen transactions in almost as many languages and dialects. A tightrope act in the bustle around him.

This seduction might not have worked at all, but fate intervenes. A self-liberated chicken darts unexpectedly in front of him. There's a tussle of feathers and a fall as spectacular as any Charlie Chaplin could ever attempt. The man bounces up to reassure everyone on the street.

'Is only a pothole,' he says. 'Is nothing. I alright.'

There is no pothole. Nobody on the street seems to notice or care. There's a chicken feather plastered upon his wet forehead. She falls in love precisely then.

SHE LIKES HIS skin drawn tight over his cheekbones and the slim bones of his wrists. She likes his chest so completely hairless even though he's embarrassed about this. She likes the musky perfume that his hair seems to exude. Is that you, she asks. No, is only hair oil, he explains. Dax.

'Say something to me in your own language?' she asks.

'You mean English?'

'No. Say something in your mother's language.'

'What you mean, girl? She only speaking English too.'

He came to this city from Trinidad, and he is one of the first to take advantage of the new Immigration Act allowing coloured people into the country in greater numbers. He arrived hoping to find some job in carpentry or construction, and he has a lot of experience, but businesses and unions are both suspicious about his skills. He doesn't care, though. He has his job distributing newspapers, and he is still intoxicated with possibility. He throws himself into the lights and vast energies of the city. He spends foolishly at restaurants, and he acts recklessly and with little foresight. He drinks the finger-bowl of lemon water at the Swiss Chalet. He treats horseradish like mashed potatoes during his first roast-beef dinner, bringing a first and massive forkful of the condiment to his mouth and shrugging off the waiter's warning about the heat. Like white people could tell *him* something about heat....

'I can't breathe,' he manages to whisper to Adele after ten seconds of silence.

'Please,' she whispers. 'Set you face properly and put you hands away from you nose. You embarrassing me....'

'I serious,' he whispers, still standing. 'I can't breathe. Girl ... I going to *die*....'

He buys himself a white rhinestone-embroidered cowboy suit and drags Adele to country music taverns and bars, places she wouldn't before have dreamt of entering. He doesn't seem to notice the people either staring icily or laughing. He waves back smiling, oblivious. He's so innocent, she thinks, an involuntary smile on her face. He's such a glorious fool.

In one wedding picture, he's sitting at a table in the basement of the church with the Czarna Madonna. He's beaming at the camera and cradling a bottle of horseradish like a newborn. She looks embarrassed, or like she's got indigestion, or like she's trying to stifle a laugh.

'Roger,' she says aloud to herself. 'He name is Roger.'

THEY ARE HERE now, and they have almost no interest in their respective pasts. Without actually discussing the matter, they agree never to wax nostalgically. But they do see old films together. While growing up in the Caribbean, each received their first tastes of escape through these films. Each studied flickering images for phrases, gestures, and postures of possibility. Bogart's smoky manhood. Dietrich's cold beauty. People who went overseas to strange lands and lived adventures during world crises, beautiful people who deserved our admiration and sympathy. Now, in a North America they had each inhabited in long before arriving, they watch *Casablanca* and *Morocco* in a new light. In an old rep theatre, amidst the rows of empty seats, silent and this time unmoved, they watch something of themselves too. Their own desires, now spectral and grainy on the screen. Distant fictions.

Marlene Dietrich: 'I understand that men are never asked why they enter the foreign legion.'

Gary Cooper: 'That's right. They never asked me. And if they had I wouldn't have told. When I crashed the legion I ditched the past.'

Marlene Dietrich: 'There's a foreign legion of women too.'

ACCIDENTALLY, and only once, they see *Nosferatu* together. It's an old film even then, and during the matinee hardly anyone shows up to watch it. Adele is gripped by something throughout the showing, her hands to her mouth and throat the whole time. She's pale and wrecked by the end and he knows enough not to ask. He's already learned about the heavy moods of the woman he loves. Only when they're out of the theatre does she offer an explanation.

'Is the expression on the creature's face.'

'You really find it that scary…?' he asks.

'No. Is not the frightfulness. Is the sorrow. Such horrid sorrow.'

THEY HAVE BOTH experienced disappointments of late. He is suddenly fired from his job as a paper distributor, and for a while he cannot seem to get a job anyplace else. He finally lands a temporary job in a furniture factory, but the work is difficult. The heated metal parts rip the skin from his hands. He either throws up his dinner or complains that the solvents and paints have made him too dizzy to eat. He'll get used to it, he says. Besides, the salary is not so bad, especially when you factor in the piecework. It won't be the last job he'll have, and the pay is good enough.

They want to find a decent place for themselves, but here too they find little success. They comb through newspaper ads looking for an apartment. They get evasive answers when their accents are heard, but they persist undaunted. They realize that their voices might be the problem, and so they practice speaking 'Canadian' to each other, laughing when the other's voice starts to pitch and lower involuntarily.

'You're singing again. Stop singing, Adele.'

'I singing?' she answers, gruffly. 'I? Is *you* the one always singing. Singing, singing like you have some song to sing....'

This doesn't seem to improve their chances. Muffling their voices over the phone, they learn of vacancies, but always seem to arrive too late. Someone else has always been there just a moment before they show up in person. Sorry, it's been rented. They continue their search, though, until they find an apartment run by a grumpy middle-aged man. He's not happy with renting out the place to coloureds, but he needs the money. They live at this house for a while, painting and doing minor repairs, waging war on the cockroaches with numerous Caribbean techniques, until the landlord approaches them furiously. Roger answers the door and the landlord doesn't mince words.

'The neighbours have been complaining,' the landlord yells. 'They don't like the smells coming from your place. They say they hear country music being played at eleven o'clock at night. They hear dancing....'

'Really, sir?' exclaims Roger. '*Country* music? Now that very odd. We from the Caribbean, you know....'

'... and they say your wife wanders about at night. They say she scares children. She kicks dogs.'

'Well, sir, that very strange too. Adele just love animals....'

'Don't play games with me. Someone has been leaving the tap running night and day. This isn't a place where water grows on trees, you know. The neighbours hear the humming of the pipes all the time. And there've been bathtubs overflowing. Leaks in the ceiling and down the walls.'

'I want to assure you, sir. We going to get to the bottom of this....'

'I don't want you to get to the bottom of this. I want all of this to stop. You don't know how lucky you people are to be here. I don't know anyone so stupid to have niggers in their place!'

Roger bites his lip and waits for the landlord to storm off. He shuts the door carefully and locks it, hoping that the landlord didn't hear the noises all the while, the humming pipe, the patter of water on the kitchen floor. He walks to the bathroom and stands for a moment in the doorway, looking at the woman he loves at the faucet of the sink. The water flowing over her hand, the thin rivulet down her arm and upon the floor still spread with mushy newspapers to soak up the spill. A patter of water to any sensible person's ears.

'Adele?'

'Hello, dear,' she says, awakening, smiling at this man, her husband.

'Why, Adele? Why do you do this all the time...?'

ON THE SECOND anniversary of their wedding, they tell the landlord that they are going away for a vacation to Niagara Falls. A proper honeymoon now that they have a bit of money saved up. They borrow a car from a friend and are admitted into a hotel on the third attempt. They are mesmerized by the gardens and falls. They get soaked with mist and end up lying naked on the hotel bed watching the sky through the window.

When they return to the city, they find their place completely destroyed. All of the furniture is missing or ripped or broken. Everything small and of value is gone. The vandals have been living inside their home for at least a day or two, since some of the pots have been used for cooking and are now blackened at the bottom with greasy bits of meat still inside. Plates have been scattered over tabletops and on floors, and one of the vandals has shit on their bed just before leaving. On the wall, also in shit, are a series of letters. G … O … B … A … C … K…. GOB ACK? A clue? she wonders. A name? Some riddle toward an identity?

Roger speaks to the landlord who is coolly surveying the mess. He tries to control his voice, knowing that they are indeed lucky to be here, but also that this just isn't right. He reminds the landlord that only he knew that they were leaving for a few days. He shows him that the lock wasn't broken, that no windows were smashed, that the thieves were confident enough to cook a meal and stay here for a while. The landlord pinches his nose and asks if anything was insured. No? Why didn't you buy insurance? What is he supposed to do if you people don't know about insurance? And anyway, was anything truly valuable missing?'

'Yes,' says Adele, 'A clock and … and … a glass and … a clock….'

'There were other things too,' interrupts Roger. 'Our wedding gifts. The cutlery the Bernsteins gives us. Your mother's earrings too, remember, Adele? Isn't that right, dear?'

'I … I don't know.…'

The landlord looks at them, nodding. He knew it all along. Cranks. Scammers. He looks around at the house once more and shakes his head.

'You know …' he begins, searching for the right words. 'You people come here. You *insist* on coming here. So what the hell do you expect?'

'WHY DIDN'T YOU tell him, Adele? Our china cups, your aunt's pearl earrings, the deya my father give me.…'

'The what…?'

WAS THIS A turning point in her life? The moment when she first realized that something was wrong with her? That something more serious than cutlery or bangles had gone missing? That so many other things were getting lost? This man beside her, for instance. Her husband. She knows his name, of course. It's Roger. But what else does she know? Where did he come from? Was he always so quiet and reserved? Did he always limp about like that, and had he always hated dancing? What at all had she loved in this body of his? His hand roughed to a glove, his calluses not content to stay there but traveling up arms and down his thighs, a uniform he wore to bed, a toughened helmet on his head. His hacking cough, his body stinking of chemicals and mapped with heat blisters and funguses.

Finally, brethren, whatsoever things are true, whatsoever things are just, whatsoever things are honest, whatsoever things are pure, whatsoever things are of good report …

'Roger?'

… if there be any virtue, and if there be any praise, think on these things.

'Roger? Where did you come from?'

'You know this, Adele,' he says, lifting his eyes from the epistle. 'You know I from the same country as you.'

'Yes, I know that. I do. But I talking before that. Where did you great grandmother come from? And she mother too?'

He knows a few things. That his grandfather could speak Tamil and his ancestors came from a place called Madras. Does this place even exist anymore? The migration happened a long time ago, and it didn't involve circumstances that anyone had thought important to remember and pass on. Origins of caste and wealth that had no business being remembered. Hushed stories of desperate flights, of cutlasses and sweat. Bodies broken in the canefields. Some surviving rituals of belief, though. Fire coal walking by his grandfather and men of his generation on certain obscure days. Songs that continued to be sung with sincere feeling even though the meanings of the words had long been forgotten. His own lips moving involuntarily to the very beginning of some lullaby right now, the language pure breath and tongue now in its ancientness and obscurity.

Araaroo ariraroo.…

'You see?' she says, interrupting him. 'You *do* know a different language. You singing that lullaby all the time.'

'Is nothing,' he says, shaking his head. 'I don't know nothing, Adele. Is just a scrap of something gone.'

THEY FOUND WAYS to believe and endure. They loved each other despite the nets of history and tradition. But it eventually died, their love. Shortly before Father's accident at work, I woke in the night to go to the bathroom. I found Mother curled up in the bathtub, shivering.

'Mother...?'

'Be careful,' she whispered. 'There a stranger in my room. And he making soft sounds like he hurt or something.'

I NEVER EXACTLY knew what Father did in that factory where he never was offered a full-time job. But once, when I was a teenager, Mother got into a panic and felt that I had to miss school in order to deliver him his lunch. I left at eight o'clock in the morning, a full four-and-a-half hours *after* he would normally wake to read his bible and begin preparations for his day. I took the bus to the factory carrying a brown paper bag with two eggs, two slices of bread with butter, a carrot and, enigmatically, a whole lemon. Maybe this was right. Maybe he liked lemon a lot. At least the eggs were cooked.

An hour and a half later, I arrived at the side door of a massive building and stated my purpose to the security guard. I received a helmet and walked through the inferno of the dark building, feeling my clothes instantly plaster against my skin, and knowing suddenly, and only then, why it was imperative for Father to begin work so early, before the heat from the machines became unbearable. I coughed and grew dizzy on the stench of the paints and solvents and the iron-tasting dust. I came to the section where Father was supposed to work and I handed the bag to a foreman and was instructed to leave.

I'm not sure if I saw my father that day, but I did notice a man in grey-white overalls and gloves, his face hidden behind a battered gas mask, glaring portholes for eyes. I was anxious to get out, for I had started to taste the airborne chemicals as if someone had daubed my tongue directly with paint, but I caught the attention of the man behind the gas mask, and so I waited for a moment. The man was working in a taped-in area, clouds of steam or fine dust around him, but he stopped what he was doing with a gun-like object to flick the switch on some machine. I remember the deepening whirr of the dying motor. A few of his co-workers looked around and began nudging each other, stealing glances at the fore-man who hadn't yet noticed the delay.

A trick, a show.

Still wearing the gas mask, the man climbed on top of the as-sembly line table in front of him. He started to balance himself on the rollers, hands outstretched but miraculously steady, one hugely booted foot placed after the other across the narrow surface, a ser-rated blade jutting up at least a foot between his ankles at one point. Steady, though. A tightrope act in the bustle around him.

He walked the full length of the table and then stooped with difficulty to dismount. His co-workers leaned their heads in to-gether again and nodded, their eyes squinting with something like laughter. The foreman just then noticed the delay and all quickly returned to their work. Except for the daredevil, who turned to me and bowed before flicking on the switch, the machine's wakening roar like canned applause.

He was my father. I'm almost certain of it.

'Do you know why she does that?' I ask.

I'm in the sitting room with Meera. The bathroom tap is run-ning yet again. The hum of the pipes, the deepening bang of water as the tub is filled. Meera lifts her eyes from her book but doesn't respond.

'Why she runs the tap all the time?' I continue. 'Why she likes the flow of water on her hand? It's because of her childhood. She was raised in a village with a tough hand pump. It required both of your hands to work, and so you only got to feel one second of water at the most when you were alone. You see? The continuous flow is a luxury for her.'

She turns a page without acknowledging a thing I've said. Her book is entitled *Radar Ornithology*, and she's an inscrutable bitch with a stupid smear of a birthmark. I hear my voice rising.

'I know these sorts of things,' I say. 'I know them because I've lived with her for a lifetime. Because when you live with anyone that long, they tell you all sorts of things without ever meaning to do so. Because she's not just some goddamned patient of yours, she's my *mother…!*'

I KNOW OTHER things too. I can remember things of great practical value. I know that Mother likes lemon and hot water in the morning. And the taste of licorice. And the touch of the silk tassel from a chocolate box against her lips. I know the sorts of things that no nurse, however qualified or sensitive, can ever imagine.

Occasionally, a memory lances me with anxiety and dread. I suddenly remember that Mother occasionally suffers from ingrown toenails, and that I alone might be aware of this. An image of Mother in endless pain but unable to locate its source, an invisible rat gnawing at her feet. Revulsion builds in my stomach as I approach her in the sitting room.

'I'm just taking off your sock, Mother. It's OK.'

I remove her slipper and sock and find that it's impossible to tell if she's in pain or if all is well. I take a nail clipper and remove small bits of Mother as she watches with open astonishment, the debris all over the rug now because in my haste I've forgotten to lay something down. She slowly lifts a sliver of herself from the floor and holds it to her breasts like a loved one, tears welling in her eyes.

'You ... *cut* me.'

'It's alright, Mother....'

'Why? Why you cut me?'

LATER IN THE evening, I stumble upon her in the kitchen spilling sugar from a large sack over wedges of lemon and then eating away, rind and all. There's a grainy stickiness all over the linoleum and white streaks on the rug leading out of the kitchen. Mother winces with each of her mouthfuls. 'Like eating lightning,' she says. She looks at the leaking bag of sugar and explains it is broken and would someone please call the ... *electrician*. She insists that the whole house deserves a good sweeping, and starts calling for the girl to give her a bath.

'I can bathe you.'

'*You* can...?'

'I can do it too. I'm your son.'

She nods warily at this. I accept the bag of sugar from her and guide her upstairs to the bathroom. I make sure the water in the tub is just right, and I add the salts. I help her out of her clothes, her hands balancing on my shoulders while I slip her underwear off. Her private skin so pale and unwrinkled, even childlike. Her elbows pressed tight against her sides.

'Don't get my head wet,' she says.

'I know, Mother.'

'I mean it,' she says, sternly.

'I know.'

She sits in the tub with the young man, perhaps her son, seated beside her. She looks slowly about without moving her head, looks quickly up at me again.

'Look, Mother. Your calves.'

'You calves?'

'These, Mother. These are your calves. They're beautiful.'

'They's not ... beautiful.'

'They are.'

'Maybe. *Some*ways.'

'Always.'

I help Mother dry herself and she laughs when I lay the towel on her head, making us disappear from each other momentarily, before pulling it off. Again, she says. And again. I help her dress in clean underclothes and a nightgown and I leave to fix her some tea. While I wait for the kettle to boil, I look at myself in the kitchen windows now darkened to a mirror with the coming of night. Are these her cheeks, her eyebrows? Are my ears really like teacup handles?

When I return upstairs with the cocoa it is to an odour that shouldn't ever emanate from a human body. An evil, metallic assault. She's soiled herself again and she's standing in a corner of her room with liquid clots running down her legs, her face breaking.

'It's alright, Mother. Let's go to the bathroom and clean up.'

'No. Go away.'

'Come, Mother. We have to go, now.'

'No! Go away. Way, way.'

'Don't be silly, Mother, you can't stay in that ... state.'

'Leave me!' she screams. 'How dare you touch me! How dare.…
What right do you have to see me like…? You hearing me? What
right?'

I move to touch her and too late realize my mistake. She begins
to scream. It's a catastrophic scream that threatens to unmoor the
very universe. There's no meaning in it at all, just the frantic pressure of air in a cracked throat. It takes me a while to realize that
her mouth has closed again, and that only my imagination still
rings. Later in the day when washing my hands, I notice that I've
sprouted little pink moons in both palms. Fingernail prints from
my clenched hands.

'WHAT ON EARTH were you doing to her!?' asks Meera, stepping
inside the front door. 'I could hear her voice all the way down the
road…!'

'Who the fuck are you to judge me, anyway?'

My outburst surprises me too. Meera looks intently at me for
perhaps the first time, a thin smile on her face.

'It's not that I was happy leaving her,' I explain. 'It's not like
I wanted to hurt her. I didn't plan anything of this. I had to get
away.'

She hangs her coat and bends to undo her laces. She arranges
her shoes neatly and heads toward the kitchen.

'You don't understand,' I say. 'You have no idea.'

'Mrs Christopher is coming today,' she responds evenly. 'We
should get the house in order.'

MRS CHRISTOPHER IS yet another challenge. Mrs Christopher

has never been married, and she has been Mother's best friend for as long as I can remember. On the first Sunday of my return, she enters the house with her own key. She quickly notices me and snorts through her nose before turning to some vague task with the foodstuffs she has brought, sucking her teeth noisily and muttering under her breath.

'It's me, Mrs Christopher,' I say, foolishly.

'M'know who it is!' she shoots back. She turns back to the food, smacking a new loaf of hard-dough bread upon the table like a baseball bat. The flower on her hat jiggling like a third eye.

Mrs Christopher always wears a flowered hat whenever she leaves her house, pausing in the mirror regardless of the rush in order to set it perfectly. She always dresses in the full-length skirts ordained by her Pentecostal church. She smells of peppermint lozenges and coconut oil hair pomade. She is a large woman with rounded arms and full breasts, though a man would be gravely mistaken to believe that there is something comfortingly maternal about her. Everything about her dress and poise has been calculated with higher principles in mind. In every ruffle and embroider, in each bone of her reinforced brassiere, there is a spiritual purpose, a steeling of the body to higher matters.

> Turn aside from man,
>> in whose body is breath,
>>> for of what account is he?

DURING HER TIME with Mother, she speaks in the most ornate country patois that she can muster, not to communicate with Mother, who speaks the language of a different nation anyway, but to exclude me from the conversation as well as berate me for my lack of culture and *airs*. With Meera, however, she is much more gentle.

'How she is with she vegetable?' she asks.

'She's OK, Mrs Christopher.'

'And she walks? She still taking she walks?'

'Yes, Mrs Christopher.'

The older woman nods and then arches her neck to glare at me from her position at the front door.

'Is she son *irritabling* her?' she says, not at all quietly.

'No more than anyone else, Mrs Christopher.'

'Well, you just call me when he get out of hand. I know how to deal with children like he, you know. He not too old to feel a woman's stick across he backside.'

'I guess not, Mrs Christopher,' says Meera. 'Unless of course he *likes* that sort of thing, Mrs Christopher.'

The older woman glares at me even more poisonously before sucking her teeth with incredible noise and leaving the house by slamming the door. Meera smiles exaggeratedly at me on her way up the stairs.

Mother has been silent for most of Mrs Christopher's visit, sitting upright and smiling weakly from her chair in the sitting room, but after the older woman leaves she beckons me with a crooked finger and whispers into my ear.

'Now *that* woman … that *older* woman there. *She* frighten me quite a bit.'

I KNOW EXACTLY one story about the two of them, Mother and Mrs Christopher. Their adventure north long before they received their landed status. It was a difficult time and a reckless adventure, two young black women in a lime green convertible which they borrowed from a young business lawyer who still owed Mother some cash for a last-minute cleaning job. He was away on vacation, Mother had tried to explain to Mrs Christopher. He would understand. Mrs Christopher, already a stern moralist at eighteen, only half believed this, but her imagination had already been seized. A journey north out of the city, just the two of them. Mrs Christopher had arrived as a domestic only a month or two before, and she was wondering when she would see snow. Would they be able to travel far enough north to see snow? This was as hot a day in August as any in the Caribbean, and they both suspected that they'd probably not be able to reach the fabled snow-line in a day. *Probably* not. But they'd maybe catch sight of a white-capped mountain or something, a snowy peak from afar. They'd maybe catch the scent of snow, a clean scent of mint and pine, doubtlessly, a mist like something rising from a block of ice. They'd find themselves reflected like giants in emerald lakes. They'd name mountains and swallow whole the energies of this land. Mother drove the entire time with a mischievous gleam in her eyes, the convertible occasionally veering right and kicking up gravel from the shoulder. Mrs Christopher leaned into the turns and tightly gripped the door handle with both hands, praying for safety.

'You have to remember is all backwards here,' shouted Mrs Christopher above the buffeting air. 'You driving on the wrong side of the road again. The left side is *suicide*. You must forget how you driven car before.'

'Is not a problem, girl,' Mother yelled back. 'I ain't *ever* driven car before.'

Soon they found themselves stuck behind a transport trailer loaded with timber, its wheels throwing up sand and grit into their car. Mother decided to overtake it. She pushed the gas to the floor with her bare foot and turned into the oncoming traffic lane, the car swaying and their stomachs turning over. Mrs Christopher had her eyes closed and Mother was smiling wildly, her head thrown back and singing 'whooooo' as the car flew past the trailer. They were pressed deep back into the seats of the automobile, sinking into the leather and becoming gloriously animal in their movements.

(The driver of the transport trailer checked his speedometer and tried to calculate the speed of the car now gunning away from him and kicking up from the shoulder a snaking tail of dust. He thought, but couldn't be sure, that he saw upon the now empty road with its liquid shimmer of heat the back of a woman's brown hand waving at him. 1963. A mirage of race.)

They had a map, but they didn't always consult it. They didn't need one, they laughed. Did they really want to find their way back? They laughed some more and this time the laugh was different, higher and tighter. They passed signs with names like Newcastle and Port Hope, Cobourg and Carrying Place, Tyendinaga and Loyalist, South Frontenac and Long Sault. They hooked a left off the highway and travelled north now, noting signs for Monkland and Apple Hill. The land unfolded before them and was eternal in its beauty. The rock was the oldest in the world and the trees were green and smart and austere.

They passed a young man with sunburned skin and long black hair who was thumbing a ride. He was an Indian, the first Indian they had seen in this country.

'Let's stop,' giggled Mother.

'Don't be foolish, girl.'

'He cute. Look at him there.'

'You don't know,' Mrs Christopher said. 'You too foolish to know. Man can't take care of you. Friends, husbands, sons, they all the same. They does leave you.'

They drove for a while until they realized they were hungry. They stopped at a stand at the side of the road and bought some jerky from an old man with leather skin. Wizened old man, selling his wizened wares. When he smiled, he showed exactly three teeth, and he pointed to a place down the road where they could get fresh peaches and something to drink. They travelled further until they came to another stand, and they bought a brand of ginger ale that both Mother and Mrs Christopher, to their shock, had recognized from their different birthplaces. Canada Dry. The white border-lines on the bottle, the provinces of clear green glass. They drank deeply of the nation and then suddenly felt exhausted, the wind blown out of them, the initial euphoria subsiding. The sun was setting over the low bronze hills and soon it was just a break-light on the horizon. The adventure was over, and they needed to head south to pick up the highway again.

But they weren't sure anymore. They wondered if they had taken a wrong turn and they realized that they should have asked the old man for directions. They kept on driving as the sun finally went under, and they had to pause for at least ten minutes while Mother searched for the headlights switch.

'Are you sure it this way?' asked Mrs Christopher.

'Of course I sure, girl.'

They drove for at least an hour before they finally saw up ahead some lights and then a booth and guard-rail, and two different national flags. It was a customs checkpoint. They had passed the turnoff. Nobody else appeared to be around, and for a while they contemplated turning back, but the road had narrowed and they had no choice but to approach.

'Step out of the car, please,' said a voice. There was a flashlight and the glint of a badge. There was another man and another who approached the car, shadows in the glare upon them.

And that's where the story always ends. Mother never explained to me how they got out of that mess. Two women between countries and belonging to neither. Two women on temporary work permits in a car that wasn't theirs, without driver's licenses or proper identification of any sort for that matter, for they had both left it at home for safekeeping. This was the early sixties, remember, and these were black women before blackness itself, before the language of civil rights or anything else that came after. I don't know what terms they would have used to explain themselves or their belonging. I don't know how they might have persuaded the officers at the darkened checkpoint to let them carry on as if they weren't from the very beginning in the wrong.

'MOTHER?'

She's in the living room, sitting entirely still and looking aimlessly through the wall in front of her. Sundowning is what Meera's books call it. The mental shutdown with the end of day. Meera is reading yet again on the couch. I approach Mother and gently take her hand in mine. Her eyes slowly focus on me. She smiles. She slowly touches my upper lip with its three-day growth.

'Moustache,' she says.

'Do you remember, Mother? The time when you and Mrs Christopher went searching for snow?'

Her face doesn't change. She moves her hand from my cheek up the side of my face and then slowly traces my eyebrows.

'Eyestache,' she whispers.

'How you both were flying that day, Mother? How you overtook that transport trailer like it was standing still? You used to tell me that part over and over. The wind and the trees and the empty land all about, flying north?'

'Eyestache,' she whispers again, closing her eyes and slowly shaking her head no, her smile vanishing.

'Is it time for bed, Adele?' asks Meera, setting down her book.

'I know you don't believe me,' I say, turning to Meera, 'but she was different then. She wasn't helpless or afraid. She was brave. She adventured....'

I can't explain or continue. Mother's eyes are closed now and she appears to have fallen asleep. Meera picks up her book but then notices my face.

'She told me the story,' she says. 'She told me many things. They were more than brave.'

THE NEXT EVENING, Meera puts Mother to bed and walks into the disaster area of the kitchen. All the cupboard doors are open and all of the counters as well as the kitchen table are spread with ingredients in various degrees of preparation. Green onions and garlic and Scotch bonnet peppers on a cutting board. Herbs and carrot tops springing out of bags on the floor, not all of them righted properly, and a pile of okra on the kitchen table. A mass of dough on the counter near the sink and flour all about the room.

'But she was upstairs with me...' she begins.

'No,' I explain, brushing the flour from my pants. 'This is me. I thought I might cook this evening. For ... for thanks.'

She bypasses the groceries still on the floor and lifts up a large paper bag from the liquor store. Four whole bottles of Baby Duck.

'It's wine,' I explain. 'Want some?'

'Sure,' she says, laughing at something. 'Why not?'

She quickly downs two mugfuls and then sets herself up at the table with a third and the bottle, watching me and downing her drinks in quick succession. I'm a bit nervous at first, but I help myself to the wine and begin to loosen up, though perhaps too much. Chopping the peppers, I get careless and chip off a bit of my nail.

'You OK?' she asks.

'It's nothing. Just a scratch.'

'What exactly are you cooking?'

'Saucy wieners.'

'Sounds exquisite.'

'It's actually pretty good. I learned it from a roommate who was born out west. He was a pretty great cook. A talent for improvising and making do. He said this was an authentic white Canadian recipe, but I never believed him. I've tried it before, but I couldn't ever match his success. There was always something missing, some rich and mouthy taste, hard to describe....'

'Umami,' says Meera.

'What?'

'Umami. It's a flavour recently discovered by Japanese researchers. It means just what you've described. That mouthy flavour. Like good mushrooms.'

'They named a new flavour...?'

'I think something's burning,' she says, indicating behind me.

'It's called caramelizing,' I explain. 'It's what chefs do. It means ...'

'Take a closer look at your pot, chef. I don't think it's supposed to smoke like that.'

'Quick! Pass me your wine!'

'Hey! Waste your own Baby Duck!'

I SCRAPE THE mess out of the pot and start again. Meera seems to recognize my nervousness around her, and she gives me some room. She goes to the record player and puts something on, a British accent, a cymbal crashing, soft feedback whine. She disappears upstairs for a while, leaving me to put the final touches on wieners and rice and salad. When she comes down, she's wearing a full-length skirt of dark cloth, and lights some candles she has found.

'You look so ... great,' I say.

'Well, there it is.'

We set plates and cutlery for ourselves on the old coffee table in the sitting room and we sit together on the couch, closer than we've ever sat before, a single candle on her corner of the table. Meera opens another bottle of wine before beginning to eat. The food is unusually bad.

'It's alright,' she says. 'Different.'

'Something went wrong. You don't have to finish it.'

'It's not that bad.'

We almost clean our plates. I pour us each another mug of Baby Duck, and I can tell that Meera, too, has become a bit more accustomed to the silence and closeness. We look sideways out the sitting room window to the moon and the lights dancing and the eerie phosphorescence of the lake, and at one point my eyes focus for a moment on the wisps of hair upon her neck. She stares ahead to a clay bowl on a shelf.

'I like those,' I say.

'What?'

'Those bowls and plates. I've seen them around the house. Did you make them?'

For a moment, I think I've blown it. A coolness enters her expression, and she leans back on the couch. She downs some Baby Duck and looks toward the window.

'Come,' she says, smiling now. 'Let me show you something.'

WHEN WE STAND, we realize just how much we've drunk. We get the dishes to the sink with a crash and then tug on an odd combination of shoes and coats before stepping outside. The moon is almost full and it lights the tops of trees and the railway track. We circle around to the side of the house where she fetches a shovel and burlap bag. She taps the shovel a couple times to remove dried clay.

'Hurry,' she says, walking briskly to the back of the house.

'Your shoes don't match....'

'Just hurry.'

She leads me toward the steep path leading down to the base of the bluffs. The moon is almost full above us and the great lake is electric with movement. The path is usually difficult to negotiate, but it's even more challenging in the night and with our drunkenness. We reach for each other for support but end up only unbalancing each other more. Each time, Meera irritably shakes her hand free, only to reach out again when the next pang of vertigo sets in.

'How'd you know about this path anyway?' I ask.

'Stop jabbering. Come on....'

We reach the bottom of the bluffs and look out upon the moonscape of the beach, white-grey shadows in the sky. Meera pulls me stumbling along the uneven shore to one side of the bluffs. She tests a spot on the clay surface with her hands and goes to work, slicing off clean pieces with the texture of chocolate, the muscles in her arms standing out.

'Got the sack ready?' she says.

'Wait....'

'Hold it for me. Here.'

'Wait, Meera....'

'The deposits here are a bit iffy,' she explains, sloppily filling the bag and dropping clumps of clay over my shoes and pant legs. 'If you really wanted to do it seriously, you'd have to find a half-decent vein. Dig it up and spread it out to dry. Crush it with a mallet then and make it into a slip with water. Strain it through a twenty-mesh sieve first, then a forty. Then an eighty if you can. Let it settle and pour off the excess water....'

She wipes her forehead, a streak of grey against her skin. Her arms are streaked too.

'It's always pretty short, or crumbly,' she continues. 'Never even tried to fire it. You'd have to try adding ball clay. Bentonite maybe. Did you know?'

'Know what?'

'The factors. Like bacteria. Live bacteria influences clay almost as much as the fineness of the grains. Clay is alive, you know. A subtle life, specific to each place. There's Grolleg from England, Florida Lake Kaolin....'

She breaks off, realizing that the bag is far too heavy for us to carry even a few feet, never mind back up the slope. We're now both on our knees dumping some of it out, Meera's skirt muddied at the bottom and hitched up to her thighs, the shadowed brown of her thighs.

'It's light enough now,' I say. 'You're emptying the bag....'

She pushes more clay back in and swings it onto her back, staggering and shaking her head no at my offer of help. I follow her up the path until she lurches to one side and drops the bag. We both turn and watch it slide a few dozen feet down. After emptying a bit more, we try again, this time together moving shoulder to shoulder, bumping slippery against each other. We lurch and sway into invisible branches and shrubs, but we make our way up safely this time. Within the light from the front porch, she starts laughing.

'You're *covered!*' she says, reaching for my face.

'But Mother ...' I begin explaining, pulling away. 'Mrs Christopher too. They'll kill us. We can't go into the house like this. We'll leave tracks all over the floor....'

'Don't be such a suck,' she says, reaching for my face again and smearing a big wad of mud on my cheek. 'We'll tiptoe around. We'll wash up.'

UPSTAIRS IN THE bathroom, Meera undresses in only two movements, her jacket and earth-heavy skirt thudding to the floor, her sweater and blouse coming off at once like a wet sock to reveal a shock of goosebumps on her arms and chest. I want to touch them, I want to be so gentle with them, but she's moving impatiently now, loosening my belt and urging me to step out of my pants. She breaks off and steps into the shower, crouching down to the faucet to start the water. The cord of her backbone, the smooth angles of her shoulder blades. I catch a glimpse of myself in the mirror fogging over with steam. An unattractive man? A not unattractive man? Are my ears really like teacup handles…?

'Are you coming?' she asks, starting the shower.

Inside, with the curtains drawn, we crush against each other, at first only hungry for the fluid warmth between our skins. We're facing each other but too close, in a way, to genuinely embrace. We stand like this for a while before she touches my fingers still balled up tightly against my stomach.

'Open,' she says.

COFFEE-BEAN OF her navel and the knotted riddle of her hair. The slick roughness of her surgical scar beneath my tongue. She watches as I kiss her body and she pulls my face up and bites gently my chin and lips. She is determined but silent throughout and never really kisses back until she's finished.

WE'RE LYING TOGETHER now on the mattress in the attic. We don't speak and in the silence the wind tosses the drapes and there is a faint rushing sound of the lake through the old clouded window. On the sloped ceiling of the room, there are shimmering patterns of lights, reflections of the moon off the waves.

'I like this,' she says. 'This period, this full stop.'

'Sorry…?'

'Here. This mole on the back of your wrist. Haven't you noticed it before…?'

'My father,' I begin sleepily. 'He once bicycled in the city.…'

I AWAKE SUDDENLY and perhaps to a train, although I no longer hear anything. Meera is sleeping with a slight frown on her face, her hand curled under her chin. I touch her eyebrow very gently. She frowns slightly but otherwise remains still. I hear something else, a dull thump from downstairs. I get up carefully from the mattress and make my way down to the kitchen.

The only light is from the open refrigerator door. Mother is sitting with her back against the shelves. She's holding what's left of an ice cube in her hands. I sink to the floor beside her and together we watch the cube melt slowly away.

'Touch,' she says to me, holding out her damp and empty palm.

'That's cold,' I say.

'Is hot,' she says. 'It burns hot.'

'You're right, Mother. It does.'

We sit there for a little while longer before she looks at me and smiles.

'Is so nice to see your face,' she says.

'I'm back, Mother. I was gone, but I'm back now.'

'I always knew you'd be back, dear. I always knew you'd never leave me.'

ʃoacawyoon

Four

AT A CRUCIAL AND early point in my life, something seeped into me. (Is that how to explain it?) Some mood or manner was transmitted, though my parents tried their utmost to prevent this from happening. Afterward, things became a bit more complicated. I couldn't always control the signals that my body gave off. I couldn't always produce the feelings that were expected of me, or else translate my thoughts into meaningful statements. At the very least, I picked up my parents' accent, including the inability to pronounce 'thhh.' I counted to 'tree' instead of 'three.' I had a 'tie' instead of a 'thigh.' To some, I couldn't 'think' at all.

My elementary school teachers treated this very seriously. One day, when the rest of the students in my class were learning their first words, I was summoned by the PA system to the special needs office. The teacher in the office might have been having a bad day because she didn't seem particularly pleased once she saw me. She immediately instructed me in a slow and loud voice to move my seat closer and to watch her carefully. She leaned forward and with exaggerated gestures squeezed her tongue against her teeth. 'Thhhhhhh,' she said in demonstration. 'Thhhank you. Thhhhhhhhank you.' Bubbles and flecks of spit blew out of her mouth. I pulled back in my seat, my face scrunching up. It was the most disgusting sound and gesture that an adult had ever made to me.

My reaction was taken to be a clear sign that I wasn't genuinely interested in improving myself. That my overall attitude to learning was demonstratively poor. The special needs teacher grew impatient at the slowness of my progress, and, later, at the stammer and shyness that inexplicably seemed to emerge. My homeroom teacher grew impatient too, for she obviously had no great desire to repeat the lessons that I had missed. Both made comments at my expense amongst other teachers and in class. Certain students in the playground mimicked these comments when administering 'nougies' and 'Indian burns,' when reminding me about the neighbourhood nuisance of my mother, or when hurling language about race and wealth. Like my brother, my interest in school began to wane. I might never have even learned to read were it not for the inspiration offered by my brother the poet. But also Miss Cameron.

Miss Cameron wasn't a teacher at the school. She was a local librarian, a bird-like woman with wrinkled scarves, wiry glasses over green eyes, and a whole lot of nose. She wore striped stockings and badly fitting second-hand dresses, and she was politely shunned by just about everyone in the neighbourhood. For some inexplicable reason, she invited me to the library where she worked for afternoons of tea and pickles, and for some equally inexplicable reason, I accepted.

They weren't just any tea and pickles. Miss Cameron brewed her own blend of tea for visitors to the library and at home she made pickles of all sorts. She sometimes brought her creations to the library to show me, though there were stern signs throughout the small single-roomed space warning against the consumption of food and presenting the threat of cancelled privileges. Miss Cameron brought in Mason jars with checkered cloth tops packed with asparagus spears or carrots or cucumbers or small golden onions, dill and mustard seeds and whole pieces of garlic swirling in the brine. She herself never enjoyed any of her creations, since she claimed to possess a weak stomach. But she would sometimes open a jar during the many slow days at the library, and allow me to carefully fish out with my fingers a succulently braised onion.

'Our secret,' she would say.

Miss Cameron had a passion for local history, something that she desperately hoped to pass on to others. While munching on a pickled carrot, I learned about the Scarborough Bluffs and their geology. I learned about the 'Toronto Purchase' of land from three Mississauga chiefs in 1787, but also how no document describing a neighbouring 'Scarborough Purchase' has ever come to light. I mostly learned about our community of Port Junction, which was established early in the 1800s when several United Empire Loyalists migrated up from the US to set up the first farming settlements to the east of the fledgling town. Within two short decades, Port Junction would boast its own commercial wharf and ship-building operations, as well as a fishing industry and two hotels. Farmers from the surrounding areas would visit to buy and ship goods. A lucrative night-smuggling network also developed, due in part to the high regional tariffs on goods such as leather, tea, and tobacco, and the lower prices that beckoned from the nation to the south. Things had happened here. It wasn't just another suburb. It was a place with a past.

'Your parents' home, for instance,' Miss Cameron said. 'Do you realize just how lucky you are to live in such a home? Don't let anyone convince you otherwise. Have you noticed the joists? The moldings and leaded glass in the attic window? Yours is a very old place. In fact, the property is actually mentioned in one of the earliest surveys of the area. We're talking the beginning of the 1800s. Of course the house itself would be younger, especially the second storey. Still, you should be on the lookout for relics, young man, especially in the basement. Misplaced books and toys. Diaries hidden behind walls and under floorboards. I'm sure there are many interesting old things lurking about.'

She had discovered many interesting old things of her own, but none more prized than a book that she had found and decided to keep to herself. The book was perhaps over a century and a half old, and it had worn paper covers and brown pages of almost tissue-paper fragility. *Our Place, Our Heart* was the title. Miss Cameron was obsessively careful about this book. She never allowed it to be checked out, and she only ever let the most trustworthy hold it or turn its fragile pages. Inside was an anonymously edited collection of local poems and songs, including one entitled 'The Scarborough Settler's Lament,' which was at least 150 years old:

Awa' wi' Canada's muddy creeks
And Canada's fields o' pine
This land o' wheat is a goodly land
But ach, it isnae mine
The heathy hill, the grassy dale
The daisy-spangled lea
The purlin' burn and craggy linn
Auld Scotia's glens gie me

Nae mair I'll win by Asti's banks
O'er Pentland's craggy cone
The days can ne'er come back again
O' thirty years that's gone
But fancy oft at midnicht 'oor
Will steal across the sea
Yestre'en I made a pleasant dream
I saw the auld country

Each weel-kempt scene that met my view
Brocht childhood's days tae mind
A blackbird sang on Toshy Linn
The song he sang lang syne
But like a dream time flies away
Again the morning came
And I awoke in Canada
Three thousand miles frae hame

'It's nice,' I told her. 'I like it. I like the weirdness of the words. Purlin' burn, craggy linn....'

'Do you understand why I've showed you this?' she asked. 'He saw himself as a stranger here. He longed deeply for his homeland.'

When we drifted apart, it wasn't for any of the reasons you might have supposed. It wasn't because there couldn't be a connection between the two of us. It wasn't because I couldn't recognize how special Miss Cameron was, or how lonely a woman like her would be in any 'traditional community' with little genuine interest in the past. But something loomed between us all the same. Something vague and yet palpable, like a bruise or soreness after a night of fitful dreams.

'Of course, we can't stop here,' she announced, struggling with a pile of books she had just ordered from a larger branch. 'Knowing the history of this place means knowing the history of other places too. History is about relations. Here. Look at these books about your mother's birthplace. You should be very, very proud. Have you any idea of how important it was as a member of the British Empire? Do you know about the traffic between the Maritime cod fisheries and the Caribbean sugar plantations of the eighteenth and nineteenth centuries? Do you realize that in 1917, your mother's birthplace produced and refined a full *three-quarters* of the oil for the entire British Empire? Did you know that her island nation was the home of some of the most important strategic and training bases for the allied forces during the Second World War...?'

Years after, when I had broken all contact with Miss Cameron, when I had abandoned everyone of my past, and when I thought myself completely anonymous in the city, I received a brown package at my door. I panicked when I saw that the return address was from a law office. The attached letter was on official stationary, and it explained that Miss Cameron had passed away. At the request of the deceased, the funeral had been private and attended only by close relatives. Donations to a support fund for victims and survivors of colon cancer would be appreciated in lieu of flowers. The letter concluded by stating that the deceased had left me one untitled book as enclosed.

There was no suspense, for I knew at once from the size and weight of the package that it could only be Miss Cameron's precious book of verse. But I was struck with a flood of mixed emotions, including something very much like horror, when I opened the first page and found a dedication written in the neat and flowing script of a bygone generation. *'To a trusted custodian.'* I couldn't believe that Miss Cameron would do this. That she would actually inscribe my name upon such a precious artifact. That she would bestow this to me in such an indelible way.

But there was another surprise. I opened the book again and flipped through some of the yellowed and fragile pages. I stopped at 'The Scarborough Settler's Lament,' and noticed something in the margin. A smudge on the fragile paper not unlike the print of a young boy's thumb. I brought it up to my nose and caught it, just barely and maybe only because I had been searching for it. The scent of onion.

'MEERA? I KNOW you probably haven't explored the neighbourhood much. But have you ever visited the small community library not far from here? Around Kingston and Fisher?'

'Exactly three doors east from Kingston, on the north side in a yellow house.'

'You know the place? Did you ever know someone named Miss Cameron?'

'She was pretty much a neighbour. My mother's home was five doors east. We never bonded, though. My mother heard she was a radical. Maybe even some sort of left-liberal, god forbid. After that, no community library for me.'

'I can't believe you grew up here. I keep forgetting that I wasn't the only coloured kid in the neighbourhood. What was it like for you?'

'Are we ready to go?' interrupts Mother. She's joined us co-

cooned in a huge parka. She's wearing yellow rainboots on the wrong feet.

'You don't need any of that, Mother. The weather is still holding.'

WE'VE ALL BEGUN to enjoy our morning walks to the beach, though preparing for them is sometimes very trying. I get Mother out of the parka, though she protests the whole while. I slip Mother's runners on her feet and struggle to do them up while she marvels at the technology of shoelaces and keeps pulling them undone. I show and explain to her the function of her turtleneck sweater, and she begins to grow doubtful. I eventually persuade her to trust me with the fuzzy noose. For a moment, her head is enveloped and her hands shape themselves into panicked claws as the material is pulled down over her face. Then her head pops through, a smile blooming on her face.

'Again,' she says.

'Another time, Mother. Look, Meera's waiting for us.'

'Again, silly.'

Outside, the sun is out and the garage doors of the houses along the main street are brassy with light.

'Goodpeanuts,' calls Mother to a man stepping out of his front door and walking to his car.

'Pardon me?' he says.

'Good ... peanuts! Uh ... goodbutterbread!'

He shakes his head before stepping into his car. We continue walking for a while, passing a house festooned with Halloween decorations. Mother eyes these cautiously but doesn't ask.

'Good *morning*, Mother,' I finally stress to her.

'Well, good *morning* to you too, dear.'

There are two ways to the shore. The first, of course, is by stumbling down the secret path at the back of the house. The second way takes much longer, but it's also much easier for someone in Mother's condition. You continue walking east and north along the curve of the main road until it dwindles to a gravel path and hooks down and under a railway bridge. We make it this far in about fifteen minutes, but now Mother stops and moves her lips while looking at some of the graffiti on the concrete foundation blocks. She looks pensive before inquiring.

'Should we call Steven Wright for a … a *blow* job?' she finally asks.

Meera laughs, unhelpfully.

'Come on, Mother. We're almost here.'

Once you pass under the bridge, there's a surprisingly large sand beach between the rearing clay bluffs and the great lake. It's the very thing depicted on the Port Junction billboard, and almost as pretty as they try to make it out. To the left, near an inlet and a stream and freshwater marshes, some geese have gathered in noisy groups for one last rest before making their epic lunge south. In front of us, the lake is empty save for two swans that bob with impossible elegance in the waves. To the right, the beach stretches away.

Our movements are slowed and thickened in the sand, and Mother clutches my hand for balance. Meera walks by herself on the wave-smoothed slope of the shore. She picks up an empty soft drink container with her index finger and thumb. She reads aloud 'Pepsi' and swings it, flop, back into the water, wiping her hands on her pants. She picks up an old Javex container and throws this back too. Mother is suddenly astonished by the waves. She lets go of my hand and approaches the edge of the lake, toeing the waters carefully and then backing away nervously with the advancing slosh of water. Then closer again and back. Again and again, moving farther down the shore and staining the cuffs of her jeans.

'You're getting your feet wet, Mother. Come back here.'

'Leave her,' says Meera, approaching. 'She's enjoying herself.'

We stand for a while looking out at the lake.

'It's not that bad,' she says, gesturing about. 'It's almost a bit like *nature*.'

'My brother used to come here to write.'

'What are you talking about?'

'He's a poet.'

There's high shrieking and laughter and I turn to look. Even at this early hour, the beach isn't empty. Three women have gathered in a group around a large driftwood log well away from the water where the grassy sand can accommodate their prams. They are so absorbed in their own conversation that they don't appear to notice the excitement partly concealed by the tall grasses and shrubs. A circle of children, a flurry of scarves and hats. A boy and girl are trying to outdo each other in the pitch of their shrieks, and another girl calls out 'Mommy' toward the group of women. She moves out of the circle and gives me a clear view.

A very white boy. Is he an albino, then? In sneakers and a windbreaker and the hanging tail of an oversized sweater, he's improperly clothed for the season, never mind the shadow thrown by the bluffs. He's playing the captured in some game, though not very actively. The other kids have tied his legs and arms with an old pink skipping rope, but the boy's face is serene and he doesn't give the faintest sign of struggle or discomfort, even as the others kick together a pile of leaves around his legs and occasionally spray sand upon his legs. He wriggles his arm free from the rope and then brings his fingertips to his mouth to chew thoughtfully. An older kid notices the free hand and reties the boy, who again offers not the slightest bit of resistance. All the while, several children run around making a loud but wordless ruckus. *Aboo woo woo wah! Aboo woo woo woo wah...!*

'Can you watch Mother for a second?' I ask Meera.

'Are you going to play parent?'

'I just want a closer look.'

The boy acts as though he is immune to the imaginations of those around him. He sits quietly as if contemplating the shore and water while the pigtailed girl who has moved away now returns, cradling something in her hands. There's excitement and a few groans of cheerful disgust. A green-furred caterpillar. The girl drapes the creature with great care on the bare collar-bone of the boy just above the rim of his sweater. The caterpillar loses its grip and it disappears somewhere in the sweater between the wool and the boy's pale skin. There are more groans and then two of the boys start pressing their hands against the wool where it might be. There is tense silence as they notice I've joined the group.

'They're squishing it,' the girl complains.

'We've caught an Indian,' announces one of the youngest boys.

'He's not an Indian,' explains another. 'He's artistic.'

'Artistic?' I ask.

'It means he don't feel nothing.'

'He's not artistic,' says another. 'He's the boogey man.'

'*Booger man!*' yells yet another. The joke breaks the tension and all the children laugh frantically, scattering off and kicking up sand behind them as they run.

I untie the boy. He's not an albino after all, just unusually pale. He's silent and not obviously thankful for his freedom. His eyes don't meet mine but they seem to be reading me peripherally. He reaches into his sweater and scoops out some of the remnants of the crushed caterpillar with his fingertips to have a look. A slimy patch of Velcro. A shudder moves through me. I take the boy's wrist and brush his fingers against my pant leg, then feel his hand curl into mine. It's cool and moist and impossibly a child's hand. A snail without a shell, a mashed caterpillar itself. I pull away.

'You OK?' I ask.

'OK,' he says in a metallic voice. I'm not sure if he is repeating me or answering my question. His face appears completely vacant. He stares at me for a while and then slowly, deliberately, brings the tips of his fingers up to his nose.

Mother and Meera are almost beside me before I notice them.

'I want to go home,' Mother says, her lower body up to her waist soaking wet.

'She fell in,' Meera explains.

'The sea loss it heat,' Mother says. 'The waves loss it salt and smell and the jellyfish done melt away.'

We walk as quickly as possible, but Mother has already begun to snuffle with cold by the time we are halfway home. The wind has picked up and the clouds have returned. Inside, I fix Mother a packet of instant hot chocolate, cooling it with milk and testing it before giving it to her. She looks at it with an expression of annoyance on her face, sucking her teeth softly at the powder that still floats on top.

'Come on, Mother. I know it's not real cocoa tea. Just try it.'

'Did he say anything?' she asks.

'Who, Mother?'

'The boy. The ghost.'

I stir her hot chocolate to get rid of the lump. I try but fail to get her to take a sip. I fix a cup of instant coffee for myself and sit without drinking any. I respond long after she would have forgotten the short conversation.

'Don't be silly, Mother. There are no ghosts here.'

IT'S BEEN THREE weeks since that evening when I returned from a walk and found Mother in the basement, and I still haven't found the time or desire to go downstairs and check things out. I don't usually visit the basement, the oldest part of the house and still essentially untouched since this place was a single-room cottage over a century ago. As a child, I imagined the basement was the natural haunt for monsters. The axe-hewn support beams stained black with age and the modern pipes and wires and conduits twisting crazily about. The sickly yellow from the dangling bulb and the stone and concrete surfaces sweating who knows what. The nameless ache in the air, the dusty light from the slit of a window. The clutter of a past never my own.

I spend only enough time downstairs to retrieve the tin of pictures that Mother had been sorting through. I bring it back up to the living room and sit on the couch, calling Mother over, but she's distracted at the moment, stooping to pick up something invisible from the floor. Stooping again and again and moving in this way about the room with dogged effort. Her other hand cradling the hidden gleanings.

'What are you doing, Mother?'

'There,' she says, stooping again.

I sit on the couch and have a closer look at the container. It was once a five-pound tin of butter cookies, and it still bears the lines 'By Appointment to His Majesty, the King' as well as a Union Jack in vivid white and blue and red. I lift the lid off. Suck of air and an old smell. Inside are lost images.

In the oldest photos, it's hard to distinguish the image from the condition of the photograph itself. Flesh takes on yellow contagions and limbs are hurt by creases. Feet and hands suffer from frayed edges and expressions fade into vagueness or duplicity. The first set of photos is in black and white, and all are of relatives that I cannot name, though their moods and postures seem strangely familiar to me. The way an elbow is clutched in a hand, the way the back of a wrist is brought up to a cheek. There's a young woman with achingly beautiful eyes, and some children with spindly limbs and slightly bloated bellies.

There are also more recent ones in black and white. A passport photo, a woman staring back at me with the lollipop effect of her large Afro and thin neck. No smile, wide eyes. Mother's face as a new immigrant. I find another photo of a young man. He's posing saucily but with a serious expression on his face, in a beige suit with embroidered stitching on the large collar. The light is gleaming off the solid obsidian of his massively pomaded hair. He looks like some South Asian Elvis.

'What are you laughing at?' asks Mother.

'Come take a look.'

She ignores me and keeps stooping down to search the floor. There are a few photos of me and my brother, both of us looking angry and feeble in Cub Scout uniforms. There is another photo of a storefront. Honest Ed's. No explanation. Another of snow on a tree branch. A bad photo of Niagara Falls, sunburst and unfocused. An older black and white photo mixed up with some of the newer ones. A boy dangling from the branch of a fruit tree. Mango Julie? Mango vere? Mango starch…?

One of the last photos is in colour but lightstruck and blurred and also with the shadow of a thumb that blots out a corner. It's of an old woman with a small boy on her lap, and it first looks as though the photographer or the photo itself is grossly at fault. There's a plastic look to the old woman's face that can't possibly be right. Perhaps a trick of shadows or poor light or even just the weathering of time on the photo itself. But the woman has in fact been burned. Her face is a mask and her skin has buckled with heat and then set into something senseless and hard. A puzzle and then an affront. The small boy on her lap is trying to sit still. He's trying his best not to panic and flee, but his face reveals his struggle. He's me, of course, and the old woman is Mother's own mother. You can't really tell from the photograph, but this was taken in Carenage, during my first and only trip to Mother's birthplace.

I REMEMBER SO little about that trip to Carenage. A tree branch blanketed with winged ants, the electric taste of some nameless fruit, the percussion of rain on a galvanized metal roof. Other things too. The sour stink of poverty. The heaviness of a history that couldn't leave. I remember a long walk along a muddy road, the stench of shallow latrines, the chicken with an ugly sore at the base of its tail. I remember the single-room house propped up on narrow pillars against the mountain, and how we entered by sweeping aside the stained canvas that functioned as a door. And I certainly remember the shock of first seeing my grandmother. The impossible face that called me a pretty boy. Such a pretty, pretty, *lovely* boy.

She was a monster. Someone with a hide, red-cracked eyes, and blistered hands. Someone who would claw her stiffened thumb across her eyes and try to smile through the ruin of her mouth. Someone who knew very well the terror it could bring to a young boy like me, and who was careful not to brush too closely near, or bring her attention too forcefully towards me. That gesture of consideration somehow the most terrible thing of all.

'She can make us the nicest things to eat,' said my mother, talking quickly through the tension of the room. 'Oh she can make us the nicest, nicest things. You think you taste coconut bake and cocoa tea already, child? You think you enjoy coconut bake and cocoa tea already? Well, you ain't *never* tasted coconut bake and cocoa tea like Mother here can make. You ain't never taste something so simple taste so good....'

Years later, I began to understand the significance of that trip. Mother herself hadn't returned to Carenage since she was seven, since the accident, since the burning. She had spent the later years of her childhood and early youth with an aunt in the capital city of Port of Spain, and together they had cleaned and cooked in the houses of the wealthy and the rapidly growing middle-class. To Mother, the distance between the two places, Carenage and Port of Spain, always seemed immense, impossible for a child or youth to traverse, just as the distance between Carenage and Canada seemed immense and wholly impossible. Recently, though, Mother had received a letter from her aunt informing her that her mother was dying. Between my parents, there was just enough money for two airplane tickets, and Mother had chosen me to accompany her. Her youngest son, the ever-asking one. So his grandmother could see. And so I would know.

I think some of this was explained to me at the time of the trip, but I don't know if I absorbed any it. I must have been no more than four or five at the time. Other details of the trip are vague too. For the rest of my life, Mother would insist that there was a blessing. That her own mother cradled sea water over my head. An old, old gesture, she described it. Older than any church or religion, older than anything recorded as history. But I simply don't remember it.

I do remember the trick.

I was alone with my grandmother in the darkness of a Caribbean evening. She bade me to sit before her while she lifted the hem of her skirt to her knee. The scents of molasses and coffee and deeper human things. The sight of her skin, whole landscapes of waste. Here, she said, cupping her hand over mine. That same walnut shell of bone on the inside of her knee. That same rogue tendon, bunching against my touch and suddenly snapping over. With a click. Our body's trick.

'My mother too,' she explained to me. 'And hers before, and hers before that. Strange bones, quarrels deep in we flesh.'

Her voice was low and soft. Her voice was so sweet.

But I also remember the old well at noon the next day. The one that Mother had always talked about. The heavy splashes of light like syrup upon my head. The smooth handle of the pump and the gush of coolness into the metal pail. I was pumping and passing my hand through the water. Pumping and passing again and again. I was rubbing the cake of carbolic soap over the hand that had touched, pumping and rubbing and passing again. Over and over, unable in any way to control my growing desperation. The stinging and the blistering of the soap.

I'm brought back to the sitting room by a loud thump and the spill of something like sand on the floor. Mother has upset a spider plant while attempting to search for something underneath it. She looks quizzically at the soil threaded with roots, but then turns her attention back to her upturned hand.

'What have you been picking up, Mother?'

She smiles and approaches as if cradling a palm full of water. She lowers carefully beside me and, above the lid of the butter cookie tin, turns her cupped hand over. Little pinprick sounds. Dozens of fingernail parings.

'I been looking all over for them,' she whispers.

It's a stormfront, her birthmark. A pressure cell. It's a gale-force warning for all other parts of her body. The hectic mass of her hair. The creases on the inside of her elbow. The mole on the back of her arm and the silk of skin upon her collarbone. Her breasts and navel and the slip and taste of the core, the deep salt core of her....

'OK,' she says, pushing my face away.

'What? What's wrong?'

'You're trying too hard,' she explains. 'You're being needy.'

'I'm being needy?'

'Just stop being so needy.'

We're in her room in the attic. We lie naked but apart on our backs for a while. I try again by putting my hand on her stomach but she pushes it away.

'Do you realize that you're eternally sad?' she asks. 'Do you know what it's like to be around someone who's eternally sad? It drains you. It sucks your life.'

I'm hurt by this. I know it.

'You're connected to Trinidad, aren't you, Meera?'

'What the hell are you talking about?'

'I mean, you probably weren't born there. You probably aren't any more attached to that place than I am, but you're connected, aren't you? I've noticed the way you interact with Mother. You understand what she says. You understand her expressions, her names for things. Not perfectly, but enough.'

'So what? My father is Welsh, and when I visit him in Newport I understand his friends just about as badly. Who cares?'

'I'm just trying to figure out what you're doing here.'

'I'm looking after your mother. She's a human being who's been experiencing a few difficulties. Perhaps you haven't noticed.'

'But it doesn't make sense. It never did. Your money situation, for instance. You hardly have any money. Shouldn't a nurse at least have enough money to buy things for her patients?'

'I suppose you've never looked into funding for home care, have you? Or palliative care in general? Ever been to a ward for patients with dementia? Ever take the time to learn about the luxuries this society provides for women with dementia? Never mind ethnic and poor women....'

'Please, Meera. I'm not arguing about anything. I'm just trying to understand. Your books, for instance. Those titles. *XML in Plain English? Exhibition and Pet Rabbits? The Yodel in Modern British Literature...?*'

'Do you want to borrow them?'

'You know exactly what I'm getting at, Meera. Those books don't have anything to do with health or medicine. They're nothing that a nurse would ever need handy. There's not a single book on dementia or its management in this whole house.'

She quickly gets off the mattress and stands naked before me while binding her hair into a ponytail. She's so terrifyingly beautiful.

'I'm not accusing you of anything, Meera. You're doing incredible work, and it's not my place to accuse anyone of anything. It's just that I want to know a bit more about you. We don't really know each other, do we? We grew up in the same neighbourhood and we've never really talked about this. We could just talk a bit more. We could explain....'

'Explain?' she asks.

Her tone makes me stop. She yanks on a shirt and pants.

'And what would that accomplish?' she asks. 'How exactly would anything change?'

WE STEP AWKWARDLY around each other for the next few days, and the mood in the entire house seems to shift. We don't go on morning walks together and Mother herself seems entirely uninterested in such a thing. I try anyway, spending close to an hour getting Mother into her clothes. We walk outside, the two of us, in an afternoon of pale light, rainclouds growing in the sky, but instead of heading down the road, Mother insists on wandering around to the brush at the side of the house. She spends some time wading through the weeds and thistles and emerges covered in burrs, her hair full of dried thistles and bits of dandelion fluff.

'Let's go back, Mother. It's not a good day for a walk anyway.'

She looks blankly at me before touching her forehead and looking up into the sky. She blinks against another drop of rain.

'Come on, Mother. Let's get inside.'

Just before she steps indoors, I take a broom and begin brushing her coat and pants. Meera just happens to be stepping out of the house, and she gestures with her closed umbrella and asks if I should be doing that.

'Doing what?'

'Sweeping your mother like that.'

'She's covered in stuff from the brush. I'm trying to keep the house clean.'

'Well, it's disrespectful. She's not a kitchen floor.'

I stop brushing and watch Meera walk across the tracks and disappear down the main road. I clean Mother a bit more with my hand and lead her into the house. The coming rain makes it dark enough this morning for me to consider flicking on the lights, but I don't, and I don't help her get off her jacket or boots either. Moving to the couch, Mother squelches through a soaked rug since she's been watering the plastic plants and they're all now overflowing.

'Do you want something to eat or what?' I say.

No answer. Sundowning again. The coolness in her, the darkness in her eyes. She is like that for a while, transforming into something else, but she wakes suddenly and summons me over. I sigh and approach and she reaches up and touches my face, traces my eyebrows. Her eyes go far and she pulls her hand back and slowly leads it up to the thin set of scars on her chin.

'Let's just get to bed, Mother.'

She moves her hand down along her jaw to her neck, her eyebrows furrowing. She bends her head slightly and her hairline slips. Her scalp comes off at the back. This has never happened before, no matter how confused she has become. Mother has never let this happen.

She holds her wig and angles her head so she can touch more carefully. I look upon her skull as if for the first time. The glistening pink skin infected with purple and brown. The corrugations and whorls like an organ exposed to the air. A brain obscenely naked and pulsing with life.

'What?' she says, her fingers fluttering upon her skull. 'What you done to me…? What you do to me…?'

I can't help her right now. I can't go to her or help her in any way. Mother turns to look in the combined mirrors of the darkening windows, her eyes squinted and then widening at what she sees. She reaches up to touch, and then she starts to weep quietly, her eyes now squeezed shut. This lasts only for a short while, too short for me to snap out of my paralysis. She opens her eyes and touches again, her brow furrowing at something truly unusual. She curls her finger at one of the whorls of crippled skin on her scalp before bringing it forward for both of us to see. There, on her fingertip, a single dandelion spore.

I SPEND FIFTEEN minutes getting Mother's coat back on and leading her to the door. I turn to put on my own coat and shoes and turn back to see her casually hanging up her jacket again.

'Mother! We're going outside. Do you understand? Outside?'

'Warm,' she says. 'It's so warm….'

'It's cold *outside*. We're going *outside*. Here's your scarf….'

The rain still hasn't come but the wind has picked up. It's strong and damp and it eats through our clothing. A blustering fall evening. It's not a good day to take her outside, since the very air seems charged with nervousness and energy. As we move down the cul-de-sac, a flock of dancing leaves and papers moves alarmingly towards us, but I pull Mother along. We reach the sidewalk of the main road, and I feel her grip getting tighter with each step of this journey. I'm unconcerned at how odd we must look to the people in the houses. The first heavy drops of rain begin to fall and we need to hurry, but Mother yanks her hand free.

'Hold my hand, Mother.'

'You. You stop following me....'

We've of course not taken our umbrellas, and when the rain begins to fall in great stinging drops, she pulls me to a stop.

'I want to go home,' she says.

'We're not going to be long. Just a bit farther.'

'Why? Why a bit farther?'

'Because I need to know. Because I'm tired of secrets.'

She doesn't move. The rain intensifies and Mother looks straight up to the sky, blinking against the downpour, then closing her eyes and smiling as if just about to laugh. I'm angered at this. I'm somehow angered by this silliness, and I pull her harder than I had planned.

She starts to scream. A cracked-throat scream without meaning. It destroys my mind, this sound beyond voice, and it takes me minutes before I notice the lights going on in the windows of the houses around us. The heads appearing in the windows, pupils in the ghastly eyes of monsters, before they roll away.

'IT'S TOTALLY crazy out there,' yells Meera. She steps inside, her umbrella still open, and sets two grocery bags down. A slump of vegetables and soft fruit, carrot-tops painting a glaze on the floor. When she looks up, she notices the woman in a grey suit.

'Meera …' the woman begins.

'You fetched my mother?' Meera says, looking only at me.

'Meera,' says her mother again. 'Listen to me, dear. Help me understand. You've worked so hard for your scholarship. We've both worked so hard. Why are you doing this…?'

'I can't believe you,' Meera says, still looking at me, a thin smile on her face.

'Meera?' her mother continues. 'Please, dear. Just listen for a moment. Why are you throwing your future away? Are you finding it difficult at the residence? Would you like a better place to stay? It's alright, dear. Nobody needs to know you've dropped out. I'm sure you can find a way to keep your scholarship. You can still be successful.'

Meera continues looking at me with the same thin smile on her face, then turns and walks to the storage room. I follow her alone and watch from halfway up the ladder as she stuffs some clothes and belongings into her dufflebag.

'Where are you going? Meera…?'

'Don't speak to me. Don't ever call my name again.'

'Honestly,' I continue. 'I didn't plan this. Your mother insisted on coming. I just wanted to ask her a few questions about you. I didn't know this was all a big secret.'

'It's not a big secret. It's my life. And it's none of your fucking business or hers.'

'I'm sorry, Meera. OK? I'm really sorry. But you weren't ever honest with me, were you? You're not a qualified nurse at all. You're just studying economics or something....'

'I never once said I was a nurse. That was you. Your own convenient belief. Your own guilty story.'

'I don't care, Meera. It doesn't matter to me. I just wanted to know more about you. I thought we could talk about things. Maybe help each other out....'

'Help yourself out, asshole.'

She bumps her head descending the ladder. She covers her eyes and begins to cry, her mouth in an open silent grimace. I try to touch her but she punches my hand away and hurries away from me towards the front door. A wave of nausea hits me. I can't plead anymore or follow her. I walk slowly to my room and sit on the bed, overhearing more muffled pleadings from Meera's mother, but no response. I hear the front door opening and see the ruffling of the drapes with the changing air pressure. Another ruffling of the drapes as the door slams shut.

I'm still sitting on my bed when Mother appears in the doorway of my room. She's completely naked.

'What wrong?' she asked. 'It look like there something wrong in you face.'

'Nothing's wrong, Mother. Please. Let's get dressed....'

'You lying, dear. I always know when you lying. I you Mother, you know. I don't have to wait for you to tell me anything. I does know.'

'Please, Mother....'

'Is you brother, yes? You worrying because he left like that without saying goodbye. You worrying because you love him. Because he you brother.'

'Yes, Mother. That's it exactly.'

Soul on Dawn

Five

I'D FIND HIM SOME DAY, my brother. It would take me a while, but eventually I'd find him. I'd probably be in a small bookstore, that dying sort that makes an effort to showcase new and obscure writers. I'd be feeling a bit self-conscious in that space, not quite smart or cool enough, but I'd stay long enough to have a good look through the poetry section. Every once in a while I'd find a book written by someone whose name I wouldn't recognize, and so I'd read a few pages and then flip to the back hoping to find a picture or some biographical information. Some poets use aliases, of course. Some might be people you've known. And some might be living closer than you've ever let yourself imagine.

I'd notice a slim book near the back of the display table. An unknown name, a title that didn't try to placate or reassure. I'd open the pages and begin to read, admiring first the clarity and freshness of the language, the reverence for plain and simple words like rain and stone and spit. I'd recognize an investment in naming the world properly and a wariness of those moments when language seems to spill and tumble dangerously. But I'd notice other things too, a father's shoulders heaving at a sink, a mother's streaked makeup and her burnt-milk emergencies. I'd flip to the back of the book and glance at the black and white picture of the author, but I wouldn't really have had to do this. I'd have suspected long before that my brother would be writing under a new name.

I'd contact his press by phone and find out about his next reading in town. Another bookstore, a 'troubled' part of the city. I'd arrive just before the starting time and choose as inconspicuous a place as possible. Four readers, all poets, all eager with youth. He'd be the only coloured boy, of course, but he wouldn't be at all nervous in his skin, and the people here, in this small place if nowhere else, would truly see him as a poet. Near the end of his reading, he'd look up and notice me silently mouthing his words. And for the rest of the reading, we'd find ourselves stealing looks at one another, the words of the other poets swimming around us, heard and unheard. We'd both linger around after the reading and we'd eventually approach each other. I'd ask him to sign my book and he'd do so silently with his new name. And then, without any stupid show of emotion, he'd invite me for a drink.

We'd end up having coffee at an all-night pancake place just around the corner. We'd have the entire place to ourselves except for an old man with a shopping bag stuffed with papers. I'd just listen at first and he'd tell me of the review he got in a city weekly. Just one modest review so far, but it was unexpected and encouraging. I'd ask if he was working on something else, and he'd tell me yes, a book-length work on either love or global capital. Maybe both, he hadn't decided quite yet. He'd tell me of his latest hope to get a grant, though these things were always crapshoots, and he'd use this as an excuse to say that he had to get going since the deadline was coming up in a few days.

We'd rise in silence without exchanging numbers and there'd be for the first time an awkward silence. And, somehow, I'd explain it all. I'd explain that I understood the need for poetry because language can never be trusted and what the world doesn't need is another long story and all the real stories have become untellable anyway. I'd explain that I understood his use of a pseudonym, since we can only ever write despite ourselves. Isn't that right, my brother? We can only ever *live* despite ourselves? I'd explain that I understood it all, even his decision to leave home, to leave me behind. I'd tell him that I had to leave too. I returned home for a short while, but soon realized that any return is futile.

I AWAKE TO nameless fears and the wind blowing ghosts into the window drapes. This time, I'm unable to fall back asleep. I hear a garbage bin being toppled somewhere outside and the furious quarrels of raccoons. I imagine a noise coming from downstairs, then hear it clearly and know enough to investigate.

Mother is kneeling by the closet at the front door. She has brought a lamp from the sitting room and has managed to plug it in. She has taken off the shade and so the hallway is harsh with light and the air stinks of something that has rested on the naked bulb and burned. She has placed a turned-up baseball cap on the floor and she kneels before this, brushing her teeth. She is brushing with a punishing intensity and she leans to spit into the hat three times before sensing my presence and turning to show me a lurid drool of blood. She turns back and continues brushing beyond anything like need or reason and then suddenly she yanks the toothbrush from her mouth and turns to stare. In these shadows, her eyes are punched holes.

I don't know when her screaming begins. I don't hear anything at first and then just a ringing which comes from my own head before growing into a horror barely connected with this woman's gaping mouth. I don't know how long the screaming continues before I'm able to find myself again. My image in a black window, some young man stooping over her.

SINCE MEERA'S departure, Mother has entered a darkened state. She doesn't respond anymore when I ask if she is thirsty or hungry. She looks aside or through me when I stand in front of her, sometimes focusing on objects outside, a weathervane on the property far across the tracks or a discarded pop can or the coils of a garden hose in the backyard. She'll watch a square of light from the window creeping all day across the sitting-room carpet and up the wall. Or the spidering of a cracked window, a passage of time invisible to me or anyone else.

'Please try one mouthful, Mother. Just one mouthful.'

She doesn't seem to know if she is thirsty or hungry. She hasn't been eating or drinking and her lips are parched and her skin when pinched doesn't spring back. Her eyes are rheumy but hold no tears. I scrape her untouched breakfast porridge into the garbage, taking a few spoonfuls myself, realizing that I need to be strong for the next little while. Just a little while longer. I set sweets in front of her such as chocolate toffees and mint crèmes and tamarind balls, her favourite. She looks at them blankly. I take one between my thumb and forefinger and put it gently in her mouth. She holds this substance like a stone on her tongue, waiting for some explanation while her own clear fluid drips from her chin. When she slowly and mechanically moves her jaw, my own mouth feels full of something old and exhausted like ash.

She can't make it to the bathroom anymore. She wets herself and sometimes senses this and is ashamed. She discovers anew the many riddles of her body, the holes in her face, the electric shock between her legs. She continues to wander but increasingly without purpose, like the automatic shifting of someone in pain. I try to take her on walks, dressing her and leading her out of the door, but when we take a few steps beyond her home she panics, her eyes fierce and distrustful beneath her hat. Those strange upright animals and the gaping sky and the crabs like leaves still scurrying about in a climate where they don't belong. The urgent advice of birds and dogs and the call of air brakes from a passing truck. She can't interpret the advancing crush of blue that is the lake and she cries for her safety. I take her hand and lead her back to the foreign nation that's become her home.

'W … WHEN …'

'Mother? Would you like some breakfast today, Mother?'

'When … is the … *when* is the … girl?'

'She's gone now, Mother. But I'm here. I can make you some eggs. Would you like some eggs?'

'Where…? When…?'

'SHE LOSING herself. She going she own way,' says Mrs Christopher.

We're in the kitchen, Mother, Mrs Christopher, and I, the mid-afternoon light bathing us in a grey haze. Mrs Christopher is standing apart from her and doing dishes, and it suddenly occurs to me.

'Were you talking to me, Mrs Christopher?'
'Who else would I be talking to, fool?'

VERY SOON, I'LL have to tell Mrs Christopher that I'm also losing myself, going my own way. I'll have the courtesy to tell her this time, because I now know what an impossible feat it is to care for Mother. I'll try to thank Mrs Christopher and express how incredible she has been, the strength that she's displayed all this time. I'll say something earnest about the strength of the black women of her generation, and she'll rightly suck her teeth at the feebleness and belatedness of this gesture. I'll notice for the first time Mrs Christopher's thinning hair and the painful swelling of feet in this woman who seems, on the surface, to be so indomitable. I'll explain to her that I'll get another job very soon and begin to send money directly from my new workplace. I'll explain that with the trickling income from Father's insurance policy she'll be able to hire herself a full-time assistant. I'll even guarantee her all of this, and try to give her a cheque to carry things for the time being, but she won't respond. I'll finally remind her to keep an eye on Mother's toenails, explaining that this has always been a special problem, something that you have to watch. Mother might not be able to communicate her pain, you see. Mrs Christopher will pretend not to hear me and walk away.

And this is when I'll snap, over the toenails.

I'll ask Mrs Christopher just what sort of son sacrifices his own life for his parent's? Just what sort of son tells himself that this is generosity and goodness instead of a form of cowardice. An evil, a mockery of existence itself?

I'll say something like this and wait. I'll wait for a response sufficient enough to send me away. Something hurtful. Some final curse.

I AWAKE THIS time to the sound of someone smashing things downstairs. I stumble-fall down the steps to see Mother in the kitchen fully dressed, her lipstick smeared red all over her mouth like a wounded clown's face. She hasn't moved for days, but somehow she's pulled the kitchen drapes closed and she's attacking a coconut with a hammer. In the dim light, the coconut has become a human head, skull fragments strewn about the floor, tufts of wiry hair still attached.

'Feeling better, Mother?'

She looks at me and moves her mouth in an odd sideways manner but doesn't answer. She takes another swing with the hammer and succeeds only in banging off a thin corner of the cupboard. The next swing connects with the target and smashes tufts of hair and fluid all over the place.

I don't have the energy to intervene. I sink to a spot on the kitchen floor to watch her, alive with physical and mental purpose. She picks up pieces of coconut without the shell and with an old grater begins to shred them. Her knuckles sliding closer to the ragged and orange stained metal but never touching it and never wasting a bit of meat. I watch her look around for other ingredients, finding them in their old places. Flour and butter, sugar and soda. She doesn't measure but pours and shakes out in precise quantities, lucid almost beyond belief. I watch her knead and see the tendons on her wrist growing taut and loose in an even rhythm.

We loved this food, my brother and I. 'Make us a coconut bake,' we would say, and Mother would smile and promise to make some when she had the time. Coconut bake and cocoa tea. Not the sickening sweetness of hot chocolate from a packet, but a real drink that has to be cooked skillfully over a stove. Its bitter-rich flavour combining perfectly with the dense warmth of the bake. The perfect food for a winter night.

'And nothing like my own mother own,' she would remind us.

But right now, Mother's lucidity comes to an end. She has managed to set a griddle on the stovetop element, and even to brush some butter on it with a piece of paper towel, but the butter stays cold and opaque on the surface. She looks at the dials on the stove and frowns at the symbols on them. She reaches out and hesitates. She cannot decide which dial to turn and it won't matter anyway because the gas has been turned off again. Mother pulls her hand away and turns to me. She opens her mouth and at first I only hear soft coughing noises from her throat. I hear it then, or think I hear it, a soft, soft whisper.

Old skin, 'kin, 'kin
You na know me,
You na know me....

'Mother?'

She looks now at me for the first time, smiling.

'Ma ma?' she says to me, still smiling. Her eyes narrow to slits and her lips pout out to frown mockingly. A little boy's whiny call, a clownish and horridly pitiful face.

'Ma ma ma ma ma ma....'

She is silent throughout the next day and the next. In her remaining days of life, she never speaks again.

'You saw a soucouyant, Mother.'

'How old is you, child? Eight? Nine? What would a nine-year-old boy who grow up in Canada know about soucouyants?'

'You were telling me, Mother. I tried to listen.'

'Well … it always nice when little children try to listen.…'

A soucouyant is something like a female vampire. She lives a reclusive but fairly ordinary life on the edge of town. She disguises herself by dressing up in the skin of an old woman, but at night she'll shed her disguise and travel across the sky as a ball of fire. She'll hunt out a victim and suck his blood as he sleeps, leaving him with little sign of her work except increasing fatigue, a certain paleness, and perhaps, if he were to look closely on his body, a tell-tale bruise or mark on his skin.

There are ways to protect yourself from a soucouyant. She's a deeply neurotic creature, so you might try scattering some rice where you think she'll pass by after her raids at night. The soucouyant will halt and feel compelled to count every single grain, and so she'll find herself caught in the light of morning without her disguise of skin. A braver person might also try batting the soucouyant with a stick as she takes the form of a flaming ball. In the morning, you'll only have to look for an old woman in the village who appears to have been beaten. Bruises upon her. Clearly the one to blame.

Or, you might try finding out where a soucouyant conceals her disguise of skin when out on her raids as a flaming ball. Cover her skin with plenty of salt and …

Old skin,' kin,' kin,
You na know me,
You na know me.

... is what she'll chant as she tries to pull on her disguise. The burning of salt under her skin. A guise now strange and painful. The suffering of a monster that deserves no pity at all.

Mother never explained any of this to me. She told me over and over again of her encounter with the creature. That time when she was very young, when the sun was only a stain on the edge of the earth and the moon hadn't yet gone under. When she was fleeing upon a path so old that none could remember its origins. An out-of-the-way path, her ankles painted cool by the wet grasses. ('The creature. It using water in a rusted oil drum as a mirror. It putting on she skin, syrup sounds and soft snaps. It gloving on she fingers when she roll she eyes toward....') Mother told me other things too, especially later, when she couldn't help herself. When the scenes and secrets were spilling out of her involuntarily. The fighter plane crashing into the Chaguaramas harbour. The smells of the soldiers who visited her mother's home. The thin blue fire on the day of the accident. She told, but she never explained or deciphered. She never put the stories together. She never could or wanted to do so.

Miss Cameron helped me. She ordered me history books on the Caribbean and especially Trinidad. She offered me meanings when they were lacking, though sometimes these meanings became riddles unto themselves. One of the books that she ordered was in full-colour and published by the Oceanways Cruiseship Company. The cover bore a picture of a black man playing a steel pan, an impossibly huge smile on his face. Impossibly cheerful colours. A white family looking on, cameras around their necks, impossibly huge smiles on their faces too. Inside, the book had pictures and genuinely helpful advice for people who planned on visiting this tropical getaway. Near the end of the book, there was a glossary of sayings, customs, and legends from that curious land. And if you were to flip through it, you'd find entries for such words as *saga boy* … *Shango* … *sorrel*.…

Soucouyant. Touch the cool gloss of that word on the page.

'Your history is a living book,' Miss Cameron once told me. 'Your history is your blood and flesh. Your history is your grammar for life.…'

My history is a travel guidebook. My history is a creature nobody really believes in. My history is a foreign word.

I WAKE THIS time without fear, without the sounds of a passing train. A still night, the digital clock showing half past two. I push off my covers and walk down the hall to check Mother's room. She's not in bed among the ambiguous lumps of blankets and pillows. I don't panic, not yet. I look in the upstairs bathroom before heading down the stairs and calling out once. I notice the door leading to the basement slightly ajar.

Of course.

The light hasn't been turned on and there's no need to change this. There's enough moonlight coming through the basement window to show it all. Mother is lying at the foot of the stairs. When I step down a bit more, I can see that she's reclining back uncomfortably, her leg in an absurd position beneath her and her head propped upon the last stair. I descend carefully and touch her.

Cold. When I lift her head I see a spot of blood. Not very large at all.

There's no need to rush. I sit beside her with the crescent moon framed in the narrow basement window, a thin scar of light. It's so clear and immediate, the moon, that you feel you could just reach out and touch it. A cold thin scar.

'So here we are.'

I'M UNNATURALLY CALM during the preparations. I call an ambulance and watch it drive up with lights flashing but no sound. I ask if I can ride with Mother in the back and they agree. We glide silently through the streets of Port Junction at a very responsible speed. During the trip I lift the edge of the sheet to see a wrist with blue veins. Just to make sure.

At the hospital and the morgue, I'm afraid of stepping on the floor. A nurse breaks a five for me and tells me where the coffee machine is. I'm alert to every noise, every sensation. The fall of coins into the chrome slot of the machine and the cup that falls at a bit of an angle before the watery brew rights it. With my second cup of coffee, I try the non-dairy whitener without sugar. With my third, both whitener and sugar. I risk leaving the hospital for a moment to find a convenience store that will give me some more change. I almost miss the mortician when she arrives.

I have at least a dozen cups of coffee that night and yet sleep through to noon, without fitfulness or dreams.

THE NEXT DAY, Mrs Christopher arrives to help organize the viewing and funeral. She makes arrangements with the bank to unfreeze Mother's account and to settle her finances. She has strong views on what's appropriate and doesn't share many of her decisions with me. At the viewing, I see her leaning over Mother's casket, wetting a tissue with the tip of her tongue and gently working at some blemish on her friend's forehead. Most of the people in the room are women from the church whom I don't recognize. Each greets me politely but firmly and, after that, do their best to ignore me. There are a few people from the neighbourhood too. An elderly couple that lived for a while down the road. A young woman, perhaps my age. She's brown and she's wearing a head scarf. I look at her, wondering who she is. She asks me if there's anything she can do.

'No,' I answer. 'But thanks.'

'I'm Amina,' she says. 'I was a couple years behind you at school.'

I still don't recognize her. Did she really live around here? I'm suddenly conscious that I'm staring.

'Um … yes. Thanks again, Amina.'

The boy I met at the beach shows up with his mother. She wears a black dress that's slightly too small for her. She speaks carefully, holding before her a knitted purse with a hole in the corner.

'I want to thank you,' she says in an accent I can't place, maybe Eastern European. 'I want to thank you for what you did at the beach for him. Some children are so cruel. They call him names. It hurts him so much. You were kind to help.'

'It was nothing,' I say.

'Your mother, she is a beautiful woman,' she says. 'Bohdan tells me how much he misses her.'

'Bohdan,' I say, looking at the still expressionless boy.

'She helped us,' she continues. 'I was working all the time. She helped us and took him in. And she never take any money for this. When I offer, she pretended. Like she did nothing. Like she never understand. She so generous this way. She so open. She was a lesson to us all. Imagine everyone house, everyone community and nation so open....'

'I'm sorry,' I say, interrupting. 'I really have to go somewhere.'

I step into the hallway and lean for a while against the wall. Amina joins me.

'Can I get you some coffee?' she asks.

'Have you seen a coin-operated coffee machine around? You know the kind? The type that gives you options and dispenses sugar and artificial whitener and so on?'

She looks at me for a second.

'Maybe at the school across the street?' she says.

'I really appreciate this.'

'You alright?'

'Yeah. Sure.'

I exhaust my pocket change after three cups but make a trip to the supermarket that evening. At home, I lay out several different brands of coffee whiteners. I also lay out several 'brewed' cups of instant coffee and a bowl of sugar. This way, I'll be able to figure out how it's done. How the taste in the machine is achieved. I keep working late into the night, my head ringing with caffeine, never quite getting it right.

The secret must be in the way it's prepared. The preparation and not necessarily the combination of ingredients. What's first, and what's second, and how it comes together that way. That's the riddle of everything, you see. That's the art and the trick.

I WAKE HUNG over and jittery for the funeral. I look into the bathroom mirror and decide that I don't have to shave. There's a mysterious bruise on my forehead. I touch it and wince at the sharpness of the pain, a dark brown egg. I have no other suit to put on, and the only one of my father's that even remotely fits me is his embroidered cowboy suit of gold stitching and glittering rhinestones. I put it on and crazily convince myself that with a plain tie it's alright for the funeral. That it's a tribute of some sort.

The sun is up, but it has rained hard throughout the night, and the parking lot of the little strip-mall church is muddy and treacherous. Two women stand as guardians at the entrance and inside the front door. They warmly greet me, failing to recognize me as the son of the deceased. I see two more people from the neighbourhood, and Bhodan and his mother already in the pews. I manage to catch glimpses of Mrs Christopher and others from the church, each so clearly veterans at this sort of event. They are chatting away and don't seem particularly serious or sad.

I'm dazed throughout the service itself. I notice a boy lighting candles at the beginning of the ceremony and having considerable difficulty doing so. I awake from some vague thoughts to the entire congregation joining together in song. Some sorrowful enthusiasm, though not altogether in synch and thus making it difficult to catch all of the words. I phase out again during the oration, this time paying attention to the neat cornrows on a woman's head. I'm awakened by another song and the service is over.

There appears to be little room in the hearse for me, and I insist on taking a bus to the cemetery, a gesture that angers Mrs Christopher. I end up arriving late, just as the pallbearers are making the last steps towards the graveyard. The rain has stopped but the grass is waterlogged and muddy, so the pallbearers are walking upon an impromptu road of planks that is supposed to prevent them from slipping. All are strangers to me, acquaintances of Mrs Christopher or else the sons of acquaintances. Each possesses completely different heights and body sizes, and together they seem ludicrously ill-suited for the task. They end up slipping the entire way, stumbling wildly at one point and fighting to keep their balance. I follow behind, keeping my distance, fearful of some final catastrophe.

I see it only when I'm closer, a young man wearing a kanga hat cocked to the side of his head and bearing a steel pan. Someone actually brought a steel pan to Mother's funeral. A panic comes upon me. Is the young man going to belt out 'Copacabana' as the coffin is lowered? Is nothing sacred anymore? I hate pan, and I can't ever remember Mother listening to it. I'm still staring at this man when Mrs Christopher steps forward and puts on some horn-rimmed glasses and unfolds a page of ruled paper.

'She liked the smell of lavender,' she says. 'She liked it when you pressed you thumbs into the small of she back. She liked tamarind candy and salt prunes. She liked the horizons on waters.…'

My mind wanders. Salt prunes. I think I had this once as a child. They're red and evilly good in a mouth-tightening, scrunched-up-eyes sort of way. My mind wanders and I miss the rest of the list and awaken to a tinny percussion that gathers into the first bars of 'Amazing Grace.' I immediately turn away from the pan player and focus on the surrounding scenery, the wet grass and the maple and birch, but I'm drawn back to the music. It's so sorrowful. I see it now. It's the most sorrowful instrument that humankind has ever created. How could anyone, including me, have failed to appreciate this truth, this genius?

The hymn ends. The coffin is placed on nylon straps suspended above the grave, and the device that does the lowering is activated. The coffin takes what seems to be an unusual amount of time to lower, but finally, judging from the slack straps and the still device, the job is over. We stand in silence at the grave and then we hear it. The heavy wet splash of the coffin finally stabilizing itself at the watery bottom of the shaft.

I giggle. I actually giggle aloud and all eyes turn to me before I'm drowned in nausea and sorrow.

THEY SERVE JERK chicken and roti and dal and rice at the reception. It's the most delicious food that I have ever tasted, and I gorge myself near the serving table, nodding silently when people offer condolences. I gorge and gorge and gorge, and then hurry to the bathroom to retch endlessly into the sink. I wipe my mouth and the splashes on my suit with toilet paper and then return to the table to gorge some more.

AFTER MY THIRD trip to the bathroom, I see Bohdan sitting alone, empty seats around him. I join him.

'Your mother is dead,' he says.

'Yes. She's dead.'

'She fell. Now, she is dead.'

'Yes, Bohdan. She's gone now.'

He looks at something just above my eyes. I turn around a couple times before realizing that he's looking at the bruise on my forehead. He reaches towards it and I lean closer. He probes gently and then moves down to my eyebrows, tracing them with his thumb.

His cool fingers before he pulls them away.

'Eyestache,' he says.

I SLOWLY REGAIN my senses in the days that follow, and I'm filled with a new degree of energy and purpose. There are a million things to do, but the most compelling task at the moment is to sell the house. Still pinned on Mother's refrigerator is a magnetic sticker with telephone numbers for emergencies or semi-emergencies such as a fire or burglary or the ingestion of poison or lapses in mental health. These numbers are courtesy of Cheryl Kandarsingh, a real estate agent. Her image is also on the sticker, an attractive young woman wearing a rich purple jacket.

She's even more attractive in person, though with a slightly distressed expression upon first seeing the house. I explain my situation as briefly as possible. I need to sell quickly because my mother died and I'm leaving very soon. Cheryl nods and immediately turns to look about, pulling out a mini cassette recorder and commenting on the foundation, the age of the roof, the wiring.

'It's of course much harder when you need to sell quickly,' she explains. 'But we'll probably still get something for it. The surrounding neighbourhood is really quite attractive. We'll emphasize that people should bring their own ideas.'

She asks if the basement collects moisture or if there are any leaks, if there's any leaded paint or asbestos insulation.

'I don't think so. I think it was built before all of that.'

'Heritage' she says, smiling slyly. 'Gotcha.'

She soon organizes a showing. A variety of people come to inspect the house, but all leave very quickly. None seem terribly impressed with the house itself or the details painstakingly added by my parents over the years, the refinished wooden trim, the careful painting, the additions to the garden outside. I try to see Mother's house for the first time, as a visitor might see it. It's old, sure, but it's been cared for. It still might make a good home. When the sound of an approaching freight train grows, Cheryl's voice becomes more urgent and animated.

'It's an excellent neighbourhood,' she tells a new family. 'So good, in fact, that when condominiums were proposed a couple blocks away, many in the neighbourhood kicked up quite a fuss and the plans were halted. People were afraid that some of the units would be set aside for government housing. That the culture of the neighbourhood would change.'

The train rumbles by into silence. The couple look about the house a bit more, and I see the man discreetly bouncing on the floor near the wall closest to the bluffs.

'Is it really a good neighbourhood?' the woman asks me.

'You get used to it,' I say, receiving a sharp look from Cheryl.

WE FINALLY SELL the house to a couple who admits that they're planning on razing the property and building anew. In the meanwhile, they'll rent the place out to university students during the upcoming winter term. They'll of course need a closing date very soon. We make several proposals, but they insist on something faster each time. Finally, Cheryl arranges the paperwork and I sign away. In less than a month, I'll have to vacate the place, a tight but manageable schedule.

I receive a cheque that for Cheryl is slightly disappointing, but for me is nothing less than astounding. $53,000. I go to the bank with it, approaching the clerk with sweating hands and fumbling with every single bit of identification that I own, including the library card that Miss Cameron issued to me when I was thirteen. The clerk looks at two pieces of ID and deposits the money and smiles and hands me proof and says, 'Next.' I'm completely dumbfounded by the balance slip in my hand. This is amazing. This just isn't right.

So what now?

Late the following afternoon, I don once again my father's embroidered cowboy suit, minus the tie. I take a bus going west toward the city, watching the evening come early to the overcast skies and listening as the languages around me multiply. High-rise apartment buildings begin to loom and the green space disappears. I overshoot Mrs Christopher's apartment and have to walk back in the thin rain and dark. I take an elevator up that smells of turmeric and garlic. Ringing the buzzer at Mrs Christopher's unit, I wait long minutes before she unlocks the door, first peeking at me with the security chain still on.

'It's me, Mrs Christopher.'

'I see that. What you want?'

'I need to talk to you about something.'

'I busy. Come back some other time.'

'Please.'

The word emerges strange and broken from my mouth and Mrs Christopher looks at me for a moment with some unreadable expression. She shuts the door hard again and there's the sound of several locks being worked before she swings it abruptly open.

'I don't have too much time,' she says. 'Take off you shoes.'

Nonetheless, she insists on serving me tea before listening any further. She waits alone in the kitchen for the water to boil. She pours two cups of water and then dips a single teabag from one cup to the other, staining both waters evenly before carefully wrapping the bag in a crinkled square of aluminum foil. I expected her home to be in extremely good order, but it's not. There are cushions on the floor and a clutter of books on the shelves. I strain my eyes but can't make out the titles.

'You looking for something?' says Mrs Christopher abruptly.

'I just sold the house,' I say, sitting up a bit more. 'I sold the house, and I want to give you some of the money.'

'You sell it for a good price?'

'Not bad. I'd like to give you $10,000.'

I wasn't entirely sure what her reaction would be. I thought maybe she'd hold her hands to her mouth, her eyes widening with excitement. I thought maybe, just maybe, she'd scream with happiness and lurch toward me to offer a hug. I didn't think she'd be like this. Silent and stonily staring.

'How much you sell the house for?' she asks.

'About $50,000.'

'Fool! It worth more than that! You get cheat!'

'It's what I could get at the moment. I had to sell it quick.'

'It not enough.'

'It's more than enough for me. It's not worth any more hassles.'

'For *me*, I talking. It not enough for *me*.'

'What…?!'

She leaves to fetch a notebook from her bedroom. She shows me the math. It's long and complex and my mind is still grappling with this unexpected reaction, but the subtotals are clear enough. 'In-home care at standard wages for 254 weeks.' (The hours of each week here written most carefully in different coloured inks.)

'General living costs for patient.' (Also broken down weekly.) 'Monies earmarked and available to be drawn out of Adele's bank account on a monthly basis for precisely these services and necessities.' And finally, 'Payment Owing.' I'm looking here at the figure: $100,344.10. She's actually included the ten cents.

And this is just the latest subtotal. Mrs Christopher flips back a dozen or so pages in her notebook and shows me headings such as 'Wages Received as a Domestic Worker with Allowances for Room and Board' and then 'Minimum Wage for Landed Status Workers in Canada.' There are neat dates beside each weekly entry, and I notice one dated 24/07/1963. Mrs Christopher then flips forward to the final written page in her journal and touches the tip of her tongue to the corner of her mouth while doing a quick calculation. Total amount owing: $345,033.48.

'You're joking!' I begin. 'The years you weren't paid minimum wage? Have you lost your mind? I'm not responsible for what happened to you in the past! I wasn't even close to being alive in 1963…!'

'Well, you is alive right now!'

'… and, anyway, it's legally my house! I don't have to offer you anything and here I am offering you a lot. For god's sake, she was your *friend*…!'

'Yes, she was my friend. She was my friend long before you was a small nothing swimming around in some man's stupid thing, so don't you remind me she was my friend. That not at all the point. You check the math yourself. Is all right and proper.'

I can't believe this is happening to me. I don't know what angers me the most, the demand itself or the fact that I expected gratitude, just simple gratitude, from this woman.

'I'll give you half of the $53,000,' I say.

'It still ain't enough. The whole house ain't enough. But if you give me fifty-three, I'll forgive you the rest.'

'The *whole*…? *Forgive*…? I'm her goddamned son!'

'That not the point either. You think you blood alone mean you ought to be rich with plenty monies? Is that what they teach you in that white-man school? I know what I deserve. You just check that math. And don't you *dare* use the Lord's name in vain in my presence, child. You mighta have money and learn high-high talk and whatnot. You mighta have a happy life with plenty food and clothes, but don't you dare talk like that in my house.'

'That's it, isn't it?' I say, nodding madly. 'You think I've had it easy. You think I haven't paid any price at all. And so you want me to pay for what *you've* experienced. You want me to pay for all the things that have happened to *you. Then* you'll be satisfied. *Then* you'll finally be happy.'

She looks coolly at me and sighs.

'No, child,' she says. 'That won't make me happy. Justice don't never make anyone happy. Is just justice.'

And so, after a pause, I agree. I agree swearing to high heaven because there's obviously no such thing as fairness in this world or any hope of reasoning with that whole idiotic generation before me. Mrs Christopher might as well have thousands of dollars to buy more ridiculous hats and iron-reinforced brassieres. More flower-scented toiletries and Pentecostal lunacy. I storm out of her place without putting on my shoes and squelch through the muddy courtyard of her apartment complex in my socks. I ride the bus home, asking people what the fuck they're looking at. When I get off at my stop, I catch a glimpse in the bus driver's rear-view mirror of an insane black cowboy. I walk home and grab my chequebook and yank on Father's construction boots and catch another bus back to Mrs Christopher's house. At her kitchen table, I write a cheque for fifty-three fucking thousand dollars and then rip this out and tear it up. On another cheque I write out fifty-three thousand dollars without the adjective and thrust it toward her. Mrs Christopher takes it calmly and silently and holds it up to a light to check for watermarks. *Watermarks!* I grab my shoes from the hallway as I leave again, then wheel to face her.

'Mrs Christopher? Just one more thing, please? Just one more moment of your precious time. I'd like to teach you something. I learned it long ago. It didn't come easy to me, but I eventually got it. I'm sure you'll be able to get it too. You just have to listen carefully and then practice over and over again. Ready? Are you ready?'

She looks warily at me.

'Thank you,' I say.

She blinks twice.

'Did you catch it?' I ask. 'You'll have to listen carefully, Mrs Christopher. Listen to the sound at the beginning. I didn't say *tank you*, like you and my parents. I said *thank you*. I pronounced the th. *Thhhank you. Thhhank you.*'

She laughs.

It's the first time I've heard this woman laugh, and it amazes me. It's unlike anything I could have imagined coming from her. It's not malicious or cynical at all, not a huff or wicked cackle, but something joyous. Something loose and free and green. Something that rolls unguarded in any way.

For a moment, it completely disarms me. Then I storm out of her house and walk all the way back home, arriving late into the night and unable to sleep. But the next day, I find myself lying awake in bed as the morning sun angles above me with its wintry light. I find myself repeating the words softly to myself.

'Thhank you. Thhank you.'

It *is* a funny sound, sort of. Teeth that way on your tongue.

I'M THROWING toiletries from the bathroom cabinet into a heavy-duty garbage bag when I hear a knock at the door. It's Meera.

'You could have told me,' she says. 'I deserved to know.'

'I didn't know how to reach you. I tried your parents' house, but you weren't there.'

She looks up at the bruise on my head. She leans to look behind me down the hall and into the sitting room where items from every part of the house lie strewn all over the floor and chairs in no real order. She looks back at me, first at my face and then down at my lapels. It's only then that I realize that I'm still wearing Father's embroidered cowboy suit.

'Are you OK?' she asks.

'I sold the house. I'm trying to move out.'

'Like some help?'

'Sure.'

I NOW HAVE exactly three weeks to get the house in order for the new owners. They'll gut the place and start all over. They'll replace the banisters and rails and pave what's left of the backyard. They'll get rid of the ivy planted during my childhood, a nuisance obstructing the windows and clogging the eavestrough.

The furniture is its own challenge. My parents had been

meticulous about maintaining the couch and easy chair, using up-holstery slips and protectors whenever possible. The new owners are not interested in keeping the furniture, so I'll have to sell it somehow. I balk at this task and decide at the last minute to donate it to the church. The women with big skulking sons arrive to pick it up, never really saying much to me, but they bring me enough home-cooked meals to last a few days. Peas and rice, chopped watercress, a stew of provisions and chicken with Scotch bonnet peppers. The proportions are massive. Meera and I squeeze the dishes into the fridge and heat up only what we can eat, hoping to stretch out the leftovers for another week.

We don't say much to each other, and we don't even try to touch. I sleep in the sitting room on an old mattress salvaged from the basement. She sleeps on the couch. Her crossed ankles, her bent wrist for a pillow. She is now too quiet and still to be truly sleeping and she opens her eyes to look back at me.

'I'm sorry,' I say. 'I shouldn't have checked up on you.'

'Please don't apologize to me. Don't do that to me.'

IN ALL, THERE'S much less to do than I feared. Mrs Christopher has already claimed for the church much of Mother's clothes and personal belongings. Upstairs in the bedrooms there are only a couple of pink lamps to worry about. There's still a mirror on my bedroom wall. Looking into it one morning, I notice some dents in the door frame behind me. I turn and look closer and realize that they're notches that record my changing height during childhood. I run my fingernail down them. A Morse code.

'We should get to work on the basement,' says Meera.

'Sure.'

Harder work. It takes me three full days to cut up, bundle, and otherwise ready the contents of the basement for recycling or garbage pick-up. I planned on saving some of the photos, but at the last moment I put them in a grocery bag to throw out. At other times, I slow down and focus too much on details. An old silver-plated spoon, now bent and useless. A recipe book with ingredients added in pencil. Half a spoon of nutmeg. Pinch of mace. A rusted can-opener which smells slightly of fish. A set of brass candle-holders turned green with age. Another box, this one of waxed cardboard and bearing an oily patch but otherwise sound. I lift a corner and see the wings of a dead moth that has been pressed into the wax now hardened into amber. On the floor, the softest white powder, its life a streak of ash.

Other unexpected things too. Tucked behind an old and unassembled box of shelves, I find a pair of shears with wooden handles and rust-eaten blades. Frozen open and thoroughly ancient. One morning, Meera steps out of the basement and into the living room bearing a crumpled paper in her hands. She sets it down in front of my untouched bowl of cereal on the kitchen table. The paper is soiled with mold and on the verge of disintegration, but I can easily make out THE GLOBE at the top of the page, as well as a few of the headlines of sections: 'Situations Vacant … Situations Wanted … Domestics Wanted … Properties for Sale….'

'It was stuffed behind a rafter,' she explains. 'Maybe used as insulation.'

'So what?'

'Here, look here at the date. November 7, 1885. I can't believe it's still legible. There's more of this downstairs. What do you think we should we do?'

I shrug, shake my head no, express something unintelligible even to myself. I carry my bowl to the garbage and throw out the rest of the sodden mush.

I DON'T HAVE the energy to sort things through. I don't have the will. Meera appears comfortable when working in the basement, but for me the dampness has started to eat through my clothes and skin. I've been feeling tight in my chest and dizzy when standing up too quickly. I lie awake at nights in my sleeping bag on my bedroom floor, alternating between nausea and vertigo. The spinning blur of the world.

The next night, I rummage through the garbage bag filled with the discarded contents of the medicine cabinet. I sip from half a bottle of some liquid medicine, its cap crusted red and brown. The label reads nineteen-eighty-something, the original patient's name smudged entirely away. I chug down the rest of the bottle and lick the crystals from the mouth of the bottle, grinding them between my teeth. I look for other things in the cabinet, and drink another unidentified bottle. Downstairs, I drink vanilla essence and half a bottle of Angostura Bitters, tasting nothing. I finish off the dregs of a bottle of rum and follow this with a barfy pull from a bottle of lime cordial. Meera stands behind me now, a look on her face.

'What?' I ask. 'What's your problem?'

'I wanted to explain. I didn't know how. I didn't think you'd understand.'

'Understand what?'

SHE GREW UP IN the shadows cast by this house. This eyesore

in the neighbourhood, this wreck of troubled lives. She grew up blocks away but within its noises and radiations. A father calling in a language of poverty for his wife to return. A mother wandering the streets and calling in that same shameful language, calling for her boys to return home. Her voice pitching wildly as if some final calamity had beset the whole neighbourhood. Her bare feet in winter. Her parka in the middle of July, her face streaming with sweat.

'It's a disgrace,' proclaimed Antoinette, Meera's mother, to others in the neighbourhood. 'It's absolutely absurd. The woman should be institutionalized. I'm not at all unsympathetic to her situation, of course. But we have standards here, do we not?'

Antoinette was different. She came from the same land as that troubled woman, but she herself was fundamentally different, and not simply because she didn't happen to suffer from such an unfortunate mental condition. Antoinette had come from 'a good family' in Trinidad, a family who was educated and comfortably middle-class for whole generations. Her parents had sent her away to school in London, where she had completed a first-class degree in economics and then an MBA. After her marriage to a Welsh sculptor, the birth of her daughter, Meera, and a relatively amicable divorce, Antoinette had been lured to Canada by the offer of a consultancy position in a dairy corporation trying to internationalize its business. She was even briefly profiled in a May 1974 issue of *Maclean's* magazine devoted to 'immigrant success stories.' A postage stamp picture of her beside Meera, then a child of five, standing in front of their small but well appointed bungalow in Port Junction.

The article didn't mention the other sides to Antoinette. The many tinkling glasses of scotch and ice that she drank when returning from work in the late evenings or at night. The chronic migraines and mysterious sicknesses. The impatience and temper that might flare up at a moment's notice, and that her daughter learned to match, both women's voices hoarse with accusations of insensitivity. The article didn't truly delve into what a black woman like her might have had to endure daily before earning some fleeting acknowledgment in a national magazine. Certainly, the article didn't mention any of the truths that Antoinette had decided to keep to herself. That her coming from 'a good family' was stretching the truth quite a bit. Her parents had owned a hardware shop in the city, and they had sacrificed immensely for Antoinette to attend school far away. Her mother had died of a severe flu while Antoinette was in university, and soon after Antoinette's father had retired early to spend most of his time with his son's children.

'Why an Indian name?' Meera once asked her mother. 'Why not something French, like your name? Or Spanish, like Jacinta…?'

No real reason. Although, many years ago, Antoinette would accompany her father on trips to a rural village of South Asians near the island's agricultural centre. While her father delivered wares and attempted to drum up new business, she would watch pottery being prepared and fired. She visited the clay pits just outside of the town where the slippery red earth was dug up and then kneaded by foot. She watched as the refined mass was shaped by foot-pumped wheels and baked in kilns that were hand-fed with wood and fallen fronds and coconut husks. Kilns that were difficult to control and could only be made to function properly through the skill and judgment passed on through word of mouth alone. Peasant knowledge that had endured the trip, generations ago, across the Black Water from India. She was struck, somehow, by the entire scene. One of the girls selling pottery was named Meera. Liquid eyes, a slip of clay on her cheek. Antoinette had promised herself to name her first daughter Meera.

'Do you think I could pass for Indian?' Meera asked. 'People say I can pass for many things. Even, in winter, a southern Italian.'

'This is the seventies, Meera. This is Canada. What you look like is completely beside the point. You have endless opportunities for wealth and happiness. Always make sure to capitalize. Always make sure to distinguish yourself.'

Meaning, especially, to distinguish oneself from such folk as the troubled family living only a few blocks away. The family that wasn't likely to be profiled in any magazine article on immigrant success stories. But in the eyes of many children in Port Junction, Meera seemed unable to distinguish herself. Perhaps these children hadn't bothered to read *Maclean's*, or else failed to grasp fully the significance of coming from 'a good family' of coloured folk. Perhaps, too, these children never developed warm feelings towards Meera's extraordinarily good grades at school, and so Meera was often bombarded with questions both serious and mischievous. Is the wandering lady your mother? Could you tell her to stop picking the flowers in people's gardens or peeing in our inflatable swimming pools? Is the yelling man your father or an uncle or something like that? Can you understand what he says when he speaks? And what about the boys? Are you afraid of the older one who sulks about and never meets your eyes? That dangerously fisted look in his face? What about the younger one? The little nigger or paki who's always bursting into tears at the slightest little name or push. Are you sure you're not related? Well, do you think he's good-looking? Are you planning on sitting beside him during recess? Maybe holding his hand? Maybe holding his dick...?

Meera never put herself into any dangerous proximities. When entering auditoriums at school for plays and announcements, she made sure never to sit in the empty seat beside either of the sons of the wandering lady. She made sure to stay at opposite ends of the playground during recess. Once, though, she learned that two classes were going to share a bus for a trip to the museum. Arriving late, she saw a packed bus and, in the window, the profile of the younger of the coloured boys. She watched a flung eraser bounce off his dark head, noticed the sole available seat beside him, and began to feel sick. She suddenly realized her chance, and started faking the most violent nausea and stomach cramps. She was questioned by teachers, and she faked even more desperately, real tears now burning in her eyes, her body gradually co-operating. She ended up being rushed to an emergency ward to get her stomach pumped, and she refused to admit that her symptoms, at least at first, were invented. Even when they wheeled out that awful machine and slid the tube down her throat.

('He says he's going to be a poet,' a science teacher once joked in class, speaking of the older son of the wandering lady, absent from classes for a whole month now. 'Are you going to be a poet just like him, Meera?'

Laughter all around her. Meera's face darkening. (Why couldn't she appreciate the joke? the teacher thought to himself. Everyone knew she was the best in the class.)

Once, she let her guard down. She was twelve and she was walking home from school when she noticed that she had let the older son of the wandering lady stray too close, and that a bunch of still older boys from the community had noticed and decided to have a bit of fun. The boys formed a ring around the two of them and said that they wouldn't let anyone go unless they saw something. The air was congested with giggles, with the disembodied heat of male adolescence, with a floating notion of what a black boy and girl should be willing to do. The older son of the wandering lady could have fought them off. He could have done something to resist, but he didn't. He pecked Meera once with hard lips, their noses bumping. There was laughter, and he was jeered into doing it properly, and he so flubbed a bit longer with an open mouth. When he pulled back, Meera noticed, for a moment, a thread of saliva linking them together. Sun-touched before it was broken.

She remembers that detail, just like she remembers the trembling of his lips and the almost perfect circuit of desire and complicity that suddenly emerged between these boys of different races. Strangely, she can't remember feeling fear or anxiety in the moment itself, even when the circling boys invited the older brother to pull her nipples hard and to grope down her pants and up into her. She remembers these things happening, but as if to an acquaintance or character in a film and not directly to herself. She does, however, very precisely remember being compelled to whisper 'nigger' to the older boy, a private message just for him, and then feeling a small shiver of pleasure by the water that rimmed his eyes and never hers. She remembers how he eventually pushed his way out of the circle, walking away coolly first, then quickening into a sprint. A black boy with legs pumping all the way back to his home. As if someone there could have helped or advised him. As if any parent born elsewhere could have understood or even begun to grasp the contradictions.

Meera used to crank-call the wandering lady.

She never for a moment believed that her calls were innocent, that they were devoid of wickedness or spite. But she never allowed her pranks to become as cruel as many of the ones that others were playing on the wandering lady, and reported over and over again, with nervous glee, on the playground. Many times, Meera's calls were just stupidly banal. Giggling requests to speak to 'Oliver Clothesoff,' or 'I.P. Freely,' and funny only because of their self-evident idiocy. And, at other times, Meera's calls appeared motivated by something approaching simple curiosity. Maybe even care.

'Hello?' the wandering lady answered, sounding as if she were speaking into the wrong end of the phone. 'Hello?' she said again, her voice stronger.

'Are you …' Meera began, trying to find the right words. 'Do you know what's happening to you? Can you put it into words? Can you conceptualize it?'

A long silence.

'I'm sad sometimes,' the woman said.

Meera heard a man's voice in the background. The wandering lady tried to reply, and Meera heard a chair squeaking on the floor and what seemed to be a brief struggle for the phone. Then an older man's voice.

'Who you is? Why you don't just leave us alone? What kind of people you is in this neighbourhood? You ain't have no shame? You have no shame at all for people suffering…?'

'Good evening, sir,' Meera said, her voice snapping instantly into a prodigy's eloquence. 'This is the Port Junction adult school program. We're calling to offer a special rate on remedial grammar classes. We've heard you might be interested.…'

MEERA SAW IT, sometimes. The grey rot on the edges of things.

The aura of menace around luxury homes and dutifully manicured lawns. The static hurt on new metal surfaces. The radiation sickness of moods and habits that none at all seemed able to escape. Meera looked at good neighbourhoods, 'traditional' neighbourhoods, places where parents might raise their children in safety, places at a happy distance from the people who don't share our values and ways of life, and she saw sadness and anxiety. She saw violence. She saw war. Her mother noticed the mood that had arisen, inexplicably, in her daughter, and she began to worry. About the time Meera spent alone. About the desperation that accompanied her studies. Studying was good, of course. In fact, Meera's teachers were betting that she would win a major scholarship for university next year. But should she be holed-up studying in her room all of the time? What was she doing, really? Shouldn't she be socializing? Why would anyone cut herself off from others like this?

'It's your birthmark, isn't it, dear?' Antoinette asked. 'People tease you about it.'

'Not today, Mom.'

'We'll get it removed, Meera. You'll have a fresh start when you finally go away. Regardless, it'll all be different when you're older. You'll see, dear. Things like that won't matter in the future.'

THERE WAS A graduation party. It was organized by a boy who was off to his father's alma mater, a renowned private school in the states. Other university-bound kids were in attendance, and, for some reason, Meera had been invited. Earlier in the week, she was horrified to notice that she was one of three graduates profiled in the school paper. An old yearbook picture of herself, her hair frizzed out like a crazy Ethiopian saint. 'I guess they needed a coloured kid for political correctness,' a teacher in another class had reportedly snickered, his students thereafter making a special point of informing Meera about the joke. Meera had decided not to go to the party, but she changed her mind at the last moment and arrived in brand new jeans that were a size too small and pinching her around the waist. The conversation turned immediately and lengthily to the prom that Meera hadn't attended, and she stood quietly while drinking glass after glass of a spiked and fruity punch. She relaxed a bit as the alcohol and sugar began to take effect. She could get through this. It wasn't that bad after all.

Someone asked her about the scholarship that she had received, and if it was true that she'd be going to the city's university. Meera mumbled something to the affirmative, which didn't seem to please anyone. Another person, a boy, asked if Meera had already thought of a major.

'Economics,' she said.

'What are you going to use that for?' he asked.

'To study economics.'

The small joke fell flat and it looked like some were offended. There was a moment of uncomfortable silence, and then one boy who had enjoyed quite a few drinks of punch began describing, in great detail, the latest 'adventure' that the wandering lady of the neighbourhood had had in his parent's trash bin. She'd be missed, the boy concluded with apparent seriousness. He didn't know if he'd ever get to live in another neighbourhood with such exotic and interesting people. Another boy agreed and then re-told the old neighbourhood story about how a bunch of youths had found one of those liveried black-boy jockey statues at a flea sale and set it up on the wandering lady's lawn. The youths hid and watched as the lady came outside and actually scolded the statue for dressing like a fool and standing out there in the cold. Still another story was shared about a prankster who did himself up in shoe polish one Halloween and knocked on the wandering lady's door, pretending to be a relative and demanding that she cook him a big old meal of 'grits' and 'gumbo.' Which she actually did, never once suspecting that anything was amiss.

'She's from the Caribbean,' Meera said, 'not the American South.'

More awkward silence. One of the youths, a girl of awesome blonde beauty, spoke up and said that she found such stories deeply distasteful, and that the actions of those boys were beyond belief in their stupidity and cruelty. In fact, she said, she doubted that anyone could really have the stomach to commit such vile acts upon such a defenseless person, and she suspected that the stories were just a bunch of unfounded rumours. Which was a shame, she continued, because it gave Port Junction a bad name. One it simply didn't deserve. 'Look at all of the coloured people moving into the neighbourhood lately. They seem pretty happy here. Look at Meera. A scholarship, for God's sake. We ought to be a little prouder of ourselves.' There was a short period of silence, after which a couple of the now sheepish youths admitted that this was a very good neighbourhood, and that it was, indeed, changing so rapidly. They'd miss it all, the old times, and they'd have to keep in touch. They'd have to get together for reunions and remind themselves about things. At least, they'd always have their memories.

Another young woman started talking. She had a reputation for being quiet and sweet, but she had finished a few cups of punch and was now speaking enthusiastically about an old cottage that her parents once owned to the north of the city. It was made of oak and teak and hand-hewn ceiling beams, and it had been in her family for three generations. Eventually, though, her father considered it too much of a bother to keep up, and, when she was ten, he bought them a modern cottage closer to the city. But she ended up missing the old cottage dearly. It was the site of her childhood, a place of memories, of swings and clammy bathing suits and picnic foods. There was a cherry tree on the acreage that she used to climb, and that carpeted the ground with blossoms in spring. She missed it all so much, and she made even Meera miss it too. She had a real gift for telling this sort of story. Of old times, of places past. She was heading to a university in British Columbia, and she had decided, before leaving, to make a special trip by herself to see the old property. She drove the full day in her mother's car, never once even listening to the radio. She arrived and noticed that, from the outside at least, it looked like it had caringly been kept. She had planned on leaving with only that knowledge, but she changed her mind. She approached the front door and knocked. And when it opened, she was struck by the absurdity.

'A whole family of darkies!' she exclaimed.

Meera laughed, a short nasal huff. She laughed at the stupidity of the word as well as at the discomfort of the teller, who was now blushing and belatedly conscious of the coloured woman's presence. Meera laughed, she knew, at something else too. Something that had flashed into sight at this going away party. Something about a whole youthful lifetime. But she stopped laughing when she realized that she was completely alone. That nobody else was willing to laugh with her or even to meet her eyes with something human. A couple of the boys were indeed laughing, though only amongst themselves. Snuffling through noses and pursed lips. Exchanging sly looks and trying their best to join the others in their polite disregard.

And, somehow, the whole scene enraged her.

There was a phone on the other side of the room. Meera approached and punched in a number. She asked loudly and pointedly if this was indeed Adele, the wandering lady, so that everyone at the party would know exactly what was happening. And then Meera offered one parting joke. Something everyone could openly laugh about. She let the wandering lady know. That her entire family had been killed. That some terrible accident had happened, and that there was charred flesh and guts that spilled like rope. That her husband and children had each tried to communicate things through melted lips and salt-filled throats, but that nobody could understand what they were saying. Nobody could hear and interpret, and you, Adele, weren't there to help. There were last-ditch efforts to save their lives through amputations and transfusions, but nothing had worked, their bodies were ruined, and what would it have mattered, anyway? Your family would have survived only to be monsters in this place, forever scarred, forever proclaiming a violence that nobody in their right mind would ever want to remember. They would have been alone with their traumas, forever alone, just as you, starting now, will forever be alone.

'So sorry....' the lady's voice came through the phone line, breaking and soft. 'Please forgive me.... I so, so sorry....'

Meera almost missed it, this stream of apologies, this strange reaction, because she was watching the expressions of those around her. It had worked so brilliantly, her call, even though she hadn't immediately understood what she was doing. Because now at least, nobody could go on politely ignoring her. Now at least, she had people's attention. Nobody was laughing at the joke, but at least everyone was looking directly at her. Each white-shocked face appalled by the cruelty.

'Please forgive me,' said a voice again and again on the other end of the line.

IN HER BEDROOM the next morning, in front of a hand mirror, Meera pushed her hair away from her right ear. She saw the bruises that were caused when she had pressed the receiver of that phone so unforgivingly against herself. She touched and felt nothing at all, and she wept for what seemed to be the first time in her life.

SHE TELLS ME now that she doesn't understand that thing called memory. She doesn't understand its essence or dynamic, and why, especially, it never seems to abide by the rules of time or space or individual consciousness. She doesn't understand how a young woman, in the midst of some small crisis, can remember catastrophes that happened lifetimes ago and worlds away, remember and proclaim these catastrophes as if she herself had witnessed them first hand. She doesn't understand that at all, or else how the very same young woman, offering only what she imagines to be a cruel joke, can in fact end up remembering a catastrophe that is yet to happen.

FOUR MONTHS ago, Meera was alone in her university dorm room, flunking out of all of her courses and unable to attend classes, unable to focus on present tasks or her future, unable to tolerate anything at all like human company. She was lying awake in bed one evening when the phone rang. It was her mother, who immediately explained that she didn't want to be a bother. She realized how difficult things were between the two of them lately, but she felt the need to tell her something. Driving home from the office, she had run into that poor wandering lady of the neighbourhood.

'She was carrying groceries, Meera. Her plastic bag broke, and she couldn't seem to understand this. Or even how a plastic bag was supposed to work. I gave her a lift home, and she told me in detail, just then, that her husband had died not too long ago and that her sons had each gone their own way.'

'Her husband … *died…?*'

'There was an accident. It was terribly violent, the poor woman tried to explain. God knows if that's actually true or not. One moment she was talking about her husband, the next she was talking about her mother in Trinidad. Look, Meera, I know that all of this may not seem particularly relevant to you right now. But it occurred to me just then, how difficult it must be for that woman. Not just because of her dementia but because of her loneliness too. Anyhow, I needed to tell you this, Meera. Because I do truly love and respect you, whatever your choices. Because in this world, it's impossible, isn't it? It's impossible without the love between mothers and daughters. It's so true what they say, Meera. In the end, all we have is family.'

Meera listened and said goodbye. She waited three more hours and dialed.

'Hello?' said an old woman, her voice as if coming from across a whole ocean.

'Hello,' Meera said. 'It's me.'

'Hello?' said the old woman again, her voice stronger now, her mouth probably now at the right end of the phone.

'It's still me. I'm still here.'

'Well, hello, dear. It so nice to hear you voice again.'

Silence between them for a while. The noise of something like a drawer of cutlery falling upon the floor.

'Are you … alright?' Meera asked. 'Are things alright?'

'Well, dear. I want to tell you. The stove won't come on. The jellyfish done melted from the shore. Also, I feeling a little bit lonely, in truth.'

'I could visit,' Meera said. 'Maybe stay a while.'

'That would be nice. It would be so nice to see you again.'

More silence.

'Do you …' began Meera. 'Do you really know who this is?'

'No,' said the old woman. 'But come anyway.'

THE TRAIN'S approaching bell and the shaking of the house. A blur of light outside. Afterwards, the dark mirrors of the windows.

'She told me about your brother,' Meera says to me now in the wake of her story. 'Your mother told me a bit about him, but especially how you felt about him. How crushed you were when he left. How much you looked up to him….'

'Nothing else, Meera. Not now.'

'You need to know this. You need to see that you were right. He visited your mother every once in a while. Did you know that? He'd bring crumpled bills of money, and each time he'd knock on the door like a visitor. Your mother told me. One day, I answered the knocking and we recognized each other and stood for a while without speaking. We had no words for each other. We couldn't begin to explain or justify, but we ate dinner together, the three of us. He was famished. His jeans and sweater had holes, and he smelled, but your mother acted as if this happened every evening. As if he was still living at home. She told your brother to sit up straight, and he immediately did. Before he left that evening, I asked him if he could bring me something to read the next time he visited. Perhaps some poetry, perhaps some Derek Walcott. I hadn't read Derek Walcott, but I was hoping to make a connection. Your brother never met my eyes, but he nodded and the next time he visited, the last time he was here, he brought the same crumpled bills of money, but also a massive box full of books. No poetry, but a carpentry manual and an Italian-English dictionary and a battered volume of the Loeb Classical Library containing four dialogues by Plato including the *Cratylus*, the one about the meanings of names. Other books too, the ones around the house, the ones you see me reading. I just wanted to honour his gesture. I needed to believe that a belated gesture could matter, if only a little. He was trying his best in circumstances that neither of us had chosen. All things considered, he really could be someone to look up to.'

The background ebb and draw of the lake.

'Do you want me to go now?' she asks.

'You don't have to go.'

A BAG OF cat's eye marbles.

A stuffed rabbit that I once loved for some reason. Jiggling eyes.

A collection of records. Something by Charley Pride. A worn 45 of 'Kung Fu Fighting.' Another of 'Stranger on the Shore.'

A relief globe that Father bought decades ago. I would run my fingers up the curved back of South America until I reached a tiny bump just off the coast of Venezuela, my parents' old home. I would spin the globe faster and faster, turning geography into a blur. It still gives off the scent of orange, my typical afternoon snack.

Also in the basement, there all the while, my brother's red metal toolbox.

'Want some tea?' Meera calls from upstairs.

'No thanks. Just give me a second.'

'Are you sure? You sound unsure.'

'I'm sure. I'm OK.'

It's locked and I don't have bolt cutters. I press at the red metal of its surface and notice that it bends slightly. I take a hammer and flat-head screwdriver and work carefully for a few minutes before gradually abandoning caution. I pry at the torn metal with the claw end of the hammer and then with my hands. My breathing becomes irregular. I look down once and see my thumbnail purple and a jagged cut on my left hand.

I've made a hole that is almost large enough for me to reach inside. I scrape my hand pushing it in and then cut it again while trying to pull it out. I work a while longer with the hammer and driver until I'm able to tug out the contents. A pouch of chewing tobacco. A pocket-sized French-Hungarian dictionary.

Also three small wire-bound notebooks. The first two have had all of their pages ripped out so that only the cardboard covers remain, thin backbones of pages still lodged in the spiral binding. The third book has quite a few of its pages intact. There's no title on the cover. Inside is my brother's poetry.

It goes on like this for page after page. One one of the last pages in the book, an attempt at a word catches my eye.

Soucu

I look closer at the page and see it. A detail so fine that it could have been missed so easily. A drop of liquid that has endured after all of these years. It's magic. It's nothing less than a miracle. I notice another drop and then another. My eyes blur. I reach to touch my wet face.

I knew this. Why such stupid emotion when I knew this all along?

MEERA STEPS DOWNSTAIRS with a cup of tea in both hands. She finds me on the floor of the basement, sitting beside an open notebook. She sits close to me, lowering herself slowly without letting go of her cup.

'The floor's damp,' I say.

'It's OK.'

She takes a soft slurp from her cup and looks at the notebook in my hand.

'He's still talented in his own way,' she says. 'You see that, right? The script itself is something.'

'It's alright, I guess.'

'And there. That's an evil spirit, isn't it? A soucouyant?'

We sit in silence for some unknowable length of time. Meera takes another sip from her cup.

'You don't have to tell me the story,' she says.

'I know.'

soucouyan

Six

SHE SAW A SOUCOUYANT.

It happened long ago in a faraway place, one morning when the sun was only a stain on the edge of the earth and the moon hadn't yet gone under. She was a young girl fleeing upon a path so old that none could remember its origins. An out-of-the-way path, her ankles painted cool by the wet grasses. She stumbled into a clearing where there was an old mango which knotted the sky with its branches. Its fallen fruit upon the ground, the slick and blackened peels, the drone of drunken insects.

Something brilliant passed overhead and afterwards a silence like glass. This was when she noticed the creature. It was using, as a mirror, some water that had collected in a rusted oil drum. It was putting on its skin, syrup sounds and soft elastic snaps. It was gloving on its fingers when it rolled its eyes towards her.

She didn't run, not at first. Even though the creature smiled and beckoned her to horrors. Even though the world wheeled about and everything became unreal, the sky shimmering like a mirage of blue.

THIS HAPPENED NEAR Carenage, a village that extended from a seaside hill down to the blue. Carenage was an old village without a plan. It had winding lanes and abruptly ending roads and houses of many different colours, each fashioned out of spare wood and corrugated metal from the ancient dockyards. Many buildings were perched on pillars of brick and concrete on the lower edges of the hills to avoid flooding during the rainy season. This wasn't a nice place, but one of waste and hard edges. A place where the city dumped its garbage, piles of it along the shore. But there was one month early in the dry season when the town was a dazzling mosaic of colour in the light of noon. The hills become rich with green and fruit becomes plentiful. The many fishermen of the town bring their boats to the wooden chapel at the water's edge to be blessed, and those participating in the ceremony wear white and step waist-high into the water and afterward feast on shark and kingfish and dolphin-fish and crab.

There is a world of strange magic around Carenage. There is Chacachacare, a haunted island off the island's easternmost tip that was once a leper colony. Miles west, there is a magnetic road where carts and bicycles appear to roll uphill. Farther south, there are villages celebrating Hosay and Diwali and Phagwa, proving that Columbus was right, that it is possible to sail west from Europe and reach India. Farther south again, there is a pitch lake where the earth wells up black and prehistoric, where those who are not cautious might sink to their fate and perhaps be recovered centuries later, a body steeped in tar and half preserved, a teabag dripping juices. And farther south once more, the oilfields and the rigs with their fires burning through the night.

In Carenage, a young girl watches as a fighter plane crashes into the sea. A solitary seaplane circles the wreckage once before returning to the military base at Chaguaramas, only a kilometre away. Time is short and accidents can only be expected. The world is at war.

'THE WORLD?' Mother once asked me.

'World War II, Mother. That's why the Americans set up the base in the old harbour of Chaguaramas. They leased the site from the British. The Americans were thinking strategically, you see. They needed the base to help protect the Panama Canal. The war in the Pacific was heating up, and to get there, American ships would have to pass safely through the canal. Also Germany was trying to colonize South America. There were U-boats throughout the Caribbean. Even in the Port of Spain harbour….'

'The Caribbean, the Carib. The Arawakian, the Arawak. The Cibonnean, the Ciboney….'

'The base, Mother. The one at Chaguaramas. I learned. It was sheltered from hurricanes, and ideal for military ships and seaplanes. Also, there were tropical staples on the island to protect. Sugar and chocolate. Coffee too. But especially, there was oil. Did you know that, Mother? Did they teach you that in the late thirties, that your birthplace was a major producer of oil for the entire British Empire…?'

'How old you is, child?'

'Seventeen, Mother.'

'And what some boy who have seventeen year think he know about oil and Empire?'

'I told you, Mother. I learned. I read it in books.'

'They does always tell the biggest stories in book.'

THE AMERICAN engineers had whole libraries at their disposal. When planning out modern roads and piers and watchtowers, they could borrow from the research of earlier empires. They consulted old books and papers written in Spanish, French, and English for information about the depths of natural harbours, the severities of currents and tropical storms, and the heights of tides. They stumbled upon curious details during this research in university archives. The fact that Columbus landed on the island during his third voyage to the New World. The fact that one of the original aboriginal groups named the island 'Iere,' which might have meant something like 'Land of the Hummingbird.' The fact that hummingbirds, at least, are still around, though their population was decimated during the early years of colonization by hunters of hat ornaments.

The engineers are not interested in archaic names for the island or hat ornaments. They need to ready the harbour for modern ocean-going vessels, and so they enlist immense mechanical shovels to dredge the shallow lagoons of Chaguaramas. The shovels cut through layers of prehistory, through the sticky tarmac and sand and down to the sedimentary rock carrying imprints of earlier seas, earlier occupations and orders of life. The diggers routinely unearth fossils of fern-like plants, giant insects, plated fish. Even in the slimmest and topmost muck of human history, relics are found. Once, the shovels exhumed the rotted timbers of a sunken galley, its anchor encrusted with barnacles and sea moss. Another time, they discovered the metal helmet of a conquistador, the dream of El Dorado now a rusted bucket of sludge.

One of the American privates doing gruntwork with a shovel had a habit of occasionally passing his hand through the mud. He used to be a farmboy in Oklahoma before the Great Depression scattered his parents and siblings to the dust roads and soup kitchens. Arriving at the site for his first day of labour, he wandered to the water made milky with the dredging. He cupped some to his mouth and dipped his tongue, but spat it out immediately, wincing and spitting again. One day, he tried reading the earth with his hands as he worked, trying to get a feel for this land. But he was scratched by something hidden in the mud, an ancient arrowhead, its poison miraculously alive after all of this time. This is nonsense, of course. No Carib venom could last so long. It's absurd to imagine that it could. But the private fell sick, and he spent a full week in the medical tent.

'Complete bullshit,' remarked a captain. 'Is this what we've got here? A bunch of superstitious rednecks? Bloody Okies....'

The truth is that the Americans faced major challenges in building and occupying the base. There were morale problems among the builders and troops, and the unfamiliar climate and food and water to contend with, never mind the disorientation and boredom of soldiers stationed far away from home. By 1943, the island emerged as one of the most important training regions of the war, with not only the Americans, but also the British, the French, the Brazilians, and the Dutch all simultaneously performing training drills in different locations. New challenges mount. Those were the early days of military aviation. Planes were hastily designed and built, and pilots hastily trained. Metal and fire rained from the sky, and not always as planned. Those were also the early days of petro-chemical technology, and the newly concocted fuels and lubricants had unanticipated effects and strengths. Once, a pilot in training crashed his plane into the Chaguaramas harbour and the explosion lit an otherwise thin and innocent-looking oil slick. The fire burned for two full days, the flames and billowing smoke observed carefully by locals miles away.

The locals presented their own problems for the base, of course. Few seemed mentally equipped to understand the logic behind the curfews and the rationing of food and the strict rules on movements. Few seemed properly appreciative of the importance of establishing a wide security perimeter around a major military base, and how even a casually lit cooking fire or candle might indicate a target for the enemy. Many blacks and South Asians had been living on the Chaguaramas peninsula for generations, and some had grown attached to the surrounding lands. The bois cano and the howling monkeys. The cliffs to the north looking off onto endless waters. Some of these locals had even come to imagine that they had some sort of right to live there. But, in a relatively short amount of time, they were all transported away under the supervision of British soldiers.

Years after the war, certain historians and community activists pushing for the island's political independence would kick up a fuss. They would argue that the American military base, still operational, remained a bitter reminder of their island's long history of control and occupation by foreign powers. They would point out the continuing arrogance and racism of the soldiers stationed there, as well as the exploitative relationships that inevitably resulted. These historians and activists also would point out that a significant number of the blacks and South Asians who were expelled from Chaguaramas during the construction of the base were never properly compensated. Many estate workers were forced to abandon their livelihoods and homes for desperately needed pittances, and a great many, in fact, received no more compensation than one-way transportation to 'approved' sites such as the struggling fishing village of Carenage. Agricultural skills passed on for generations were suddenly useless. Extended kinship links were broken, and surviving families were plunged into new forms of poverty without trusted networks of support.

But other historians would offer what they described as a more 'balanced' perspective on these events. After all, the world was at war, and proper measures needed to be taken, even if this meant inconveniencing a few illiterates who, most likely, would not have grasped the severity of the situation, had it been explained to them. And, in any event, the American presence appeared to offer genuine benefits to at least some of the local inhabitants. Those eking out a meagre living on struggling plantations had the chance to earn Yankee dollars as road workers, maids, and latrine diggers. Others who had already benefited from a rigorous colonial schooling had the chance to become skilled construction workers, or secretaries, or even entrepreneurs in their own right. Some crafty locals even managed, on occasion, to fleece the Yankees of money in the rapidly growing nightclub and gambling scenes. The legacy of the base might in fact be rather more complicated and ironic than some have supposed. People trapped in the aftermath of slavery and colonialism had the chance to encounter the modern world, and to find their place in it.

RUM AND Coca-Cola,
Go down Point Cumana,
Both mother and daughter,
Working for the Yankee Dollar....

'What was that?' Mother said, noticing me just then. 'What I was singing?'

I was seventeen. I had had enough. I was leaving her, and I was trying to explain this decision. I was trying to explain all sorts of things. I wanted to settle the past. Mother was all the while humming to herself and ironing a shirt. Drifting alone while my words fell about the room empty and meaningless. Mother started to sing aloud, and the sound of her own voice seemed to startle her awake. She froze with the iron still on the shirt. She looked at me and asked.

'It's an old song, Mother,' I answered.

'A song?'

'A calypso. By someone named Lord Invader.'

She stopped to think. The smell of burning cotton started to lift in the air.

'How you know such a silly, silly song?'

'You told me, Mother.'

The smell of burning cotton got worse. Neither of us moved.

'What else I tell you?' she asked.

THERE WAS ONCE a girl named Adele. She was the sort of girl who always seemed to be elsewhere. She never had time for ordinary goals and matters, or else too much time for the ordinary. At markets, she would roam aimlessly among the fruits and vegetables, touching this and that and smiling dreamily. She would be found haunting a neighbour's window with her eyes closed, taking in the yeasty smell of new bread or the coughing stench of blackened peppers. The same dreamy expression on her face when sampling the sweet slipperiness of a chenete or the pucker of a salt prune. Or standing at the village pipe with its cool gush of water upon her bare feet and hands. Pumping and waiting for the sensation, over and over again. The cold weight and flow through her fingers. The dropping away ... the liquidity of this freedom....

'Damn it, girl,' said the man waiting behind her with a bucket. 'You think people have all day to wait for you dreaming? You think that any amount of water ever going to wash away the filth that going on in you mother two by four mash-up house...?'

SHE HAD ARRIVED in Carenage with her mother, the old woman, and a handful of others only a year ago. They were among the last of the people displaced from the estates to the north for the base's security perimeter, but they weren't eligible for any compensation since they appeared unattached to any adult man. Arriving exhausted in the village after a long journey, they were offered a temporary place to sleep only out of respect and fear for the old woman. The knowledge she possessed, the skill she exhibited in healing a boy who had become ill during the journey....

Shado beni for consumption.

Kooze maho for stomach ache.

Verveine for boils.

Mami apple for head lice.

The old woman had long memories and the proper names for things. She knew the meaning of Chaguaramas itself. Named after the palms that used to line its beaches. Named by a people who had been scattered by exploding weapons, by sicknesses that burst in pustules upon their skin. They were dispersed, these people, but their voice still haunted the place. Chaguaramas. The old woman knew the meanings of other names too. Carenage, for instance.

Named after the Spanish ships which anchored there long ago to be careened. Cleaned of barnacles and made sleek and efficient again after the trips from Africa.

'What were they carrying?' Adele once asked.

'Ghosts,' the old woman answered, a smile of exactly five white teeth.

Most of all, the old woman could heal, a skill she had inherited from a long line of knowledgeable women. In Carenage, she found a regular patient, a man named Irvine who trusted her magic, and who always arrived at her door with cuts all over him, this one here splitting his left nipple. A knife-fight, he announced to the old woman, though she knew like everyone else that he'd accidentally hooked himself again. He had worked his whole life as a fisherman in Carenage, but he simply wasn't meant to be one. The sea water assaulted his arms and legs with boils, and the sun leeched the sight from his eyes. As the old woman applied a poultice of herbs, Irvine described some of his catches. Parrot fish and grunts. Wahoo and dolphin fish. Blue doctor fish....

'So much living flesh in the sea,' he used to say.

'And endless floors of bone,' she answered.

IRVINE HAD A daughter named Joy, a girl of flawless skin and almond eyes and something else, something free and beautiful in the way she walked or gestured when speaking. There was an eternal restlessness within her, a restlessness that Adele, her friend, recognized too. At twelve, Joy told Adele that she felt too big for Carenage. Joy swore that they would somehow get away and never come back to this fish-stinking place. Irvine sensed the dissatisfaction of his daughter and tried to appease her by making long treks to the city for the small things he could afford. A cheap but new pair of shoes, a faded dress of raw silk.

It wasn't enough and Joy became impatient. She told Adele that she was leaving, and she disappeared one night. Irvine was worried sick. Days later, Joy returned, but she seemed changed, unusually shy and irritable. Then Irvine noticed the rust of old blood on her dress. He found his cutlass and ran out of the village. To do what? To run west and attack a city full of rich and light-skinned men? To run east and attack a military base full of white soldiers? And for what? For whose honour, anyway? There were no answers to these questions. He never returned.

Adele ran too, but for the old woman.

Stinking Suzy for toothache.

Ditay payee as eyewash.

Mapurite for private diseases.

And Zwill Root for bringing on a stubborn monthly blood. A foul and heavy syrup that immediately brought on cramps and did the work the girl wanted.

The old woman of the village could do so much. She could treat consumption. She could start and stop bleeding. She could patch a wound with spider webs. She knew so many things. But she had limits. She couldn't do much against the ancient moods of terror and sorrow. And she couldn't do much at all, really, against the banality of evil.

ADELE IS NOT supposed to notice. She's not supposed to ask questions when her mother returns home in the dark of morning. She's not supposed to wonder about the smells that linger on her mother's dresses. Aftershave or sweat, sometimes that most curious smell of the soldiers, something like dampened chicken. Adele never draws attention to bruises that appear upon her mother after certain nights, dark blossoms upon her neck or upper arms or between her thighs. And Adele never breaks the rules when, in unusual cases, the soldiers return with her mother. Adele always lies as if asleep on her cot, her back to the sounds coming from her mother's bed. Hurt sounds in the throat. Creatures who enter in the night and ravage the flesh....

'... LA DIABLESSE, the lady with a cow foot and the face of a corpse. The Douens who is children that die before they get baptize. They feet twisted backwards, afterbirth streaming over they bodies....'

'Are you still listening to me, Mother? I'm not talking about superstitions. I'm leaving you now, but I'm telling you what I know, what you accidentally told me...'

'... and that's why, child. Why you must always speak the proper rites. Why nothing dead can lie still without the proper rites. And why you must always curl you body away from the evil at night.'

BUT ONE NIGHT, Adele looked back. There was the sound of someone entering, the smell of aftershave and chicken and a deep voice saying alright, but almost nothing else. Adele wondered at this silence and she rolled ever so quietly to look. She saw, in a shaft of moonlight, her mother straddled atop a man and looking out of the window as if lightly daydreaming. Beneath her was a man who seemed to be holding his breath, his face pink-purple and contorted in something like pain. His eyes locked suddenly on hers, and

Adele saw something truly puzzling. Something she never would have imagined on a million, million faces like his. Something almost like shame.

ONE DAY, ADELE'S mother comes home in a bad way. She has made no money this night, and her dress is torn. One eye is badly blackened and the parts of her mouth either swollen or burst. It's worse than ever before, but Adele knows not to ask. Adele sits quietly on her cot, combing the blonde hair of an American doll while her mother tries for hours to conceal her state with makeup. Her mother leaves again the next evening, but she returns home empty-handed. She can't be bought in this condition, not with ruin so naked upon her. She tries the next night again to no avail. The neighbours in Carenage have long been disgusted by this display, by the depravity of this country woman, and by the example she is offering to her child. None will lend her any help during the lean week. No handful of rationed meat, no oil or salt, no simple meal of ground provisions.

'I hungry, Mother,' said Adele.

'Hush, child,' said her mother, smudging her eyeshadow. Her hand shaking.

'I can't help it. I hungry.'

'Hush, child. Hush, hush, hush....'

By the end of the week, they are living on diluted doses of sugar water and bananas so green with tongue cleaving tackiness that they immediately bloat their stomachs and send them running to the latrine. Adele's mother begins living outside of herself. She starts wearing her best dress inside the house, an old chiffon bridal gown that she bought in the city, her costume for work. She obsesses over her bruises in the mirror, chanting obscenities, softly naming invisible beings and events. She plucks her eyebrows until there is nothing left. She attacks her greased hair with an overheated hot comb. The sizzling unfelt, the stench of burning hair.

'Mother…,' Adele calls.

'Hush, child!'

One day, Adele comes home to find a sloughed form on the floor, her mother's empty dress. Adele looks up and sees her mother standing naked in the galvanized tub that they use for baths, the damage in plain sight. Her mother is still holding a pair of scissors to the ragged wounds on her wrists. There is blood rivering down her arms, and she is just about to sit down into her warm coffin when she notices her daughter. There is a moment of indecision, a moment of glassy stillness, when neither seems to know what to do or feel. Then the clatter of metal on the floor and that naked figure calling out. Calling Adele. Some sweetness, some hopeless longing in voicing that name.

Later, Adele visits the old woman to borrow wheat flour and oil and sugar, explaining that this is the last time that she'll do so, the very last time. The old woman stifles a bitter laugh until she sees the girl's eyes, and then adds a coconut to all Adele has requested as well as ingredients for tea. At home, Adele and her mother break the coconut and knead the ingredients into a bake. They fix the cocoa tea. They eat silently in front of a candle, flickering shadows about them.

'It was an accident,' Adele's mother explains.

'Yes, Mother.'

'Accidents happen.'

'I know, Mother.'

SOMETIMES, THROUGHOUT the island, air sirens would wail. Lights would have to be extinguished and blinds drawn. Late one evening, Adele is caught alone on the road leading to the village, a jug of milk balanced neatly on her head. She is travelling from the dairies for her mother, and in typical fashion she has wandered dreamily before realizing how late it has become. There is the noise of an engine behind her and two soldiers in a jeep yell at her to get off the road and jump into the gutter and put her hands over her head in case a bomb falls. Adele does as she is told, listening to the sirens and peeking up occasionally at the soldiers who aim their rifles up into an indigo sky cut many times with searchlights. There's no plane. There never is. Adele wonders what good a rifle would do if there ever was a plane. When the alarm subsides, one of the soldiers helps her settle the jug of milk back on her head.

'It's OK,' he says. 'You're safe now.'

The soldier looks again and his eyes lock suddenly on hers. The expression on his face changes into something vague. The soldier searches his pockets while glancing a couple of times at Adele, quick flicks of his eyes. He shakes out a cigarette from a package and lights it. He draws the smoke in heavily, closes the lid on his lighter, and then, noticing the gaze of the girl on this metal object, passes it to her.

'What do you say?' calls the other soldier, already in the jeep.

The first soldier takes another drag of his cigarette and cups his hand over Adele's, showing the girl how to hold it and click. Here, try again. Click. Click. She can't make it work. She hands it back and he smiles and then, searching his pockets again, removes something and presses it into her hand, a folded piece of paper. When Adele unfolds it, she sees that it's an American dollar bill.

'Hey nigger-girl!' shouts the other soldier, impatient at the delay. 'The Okie's talking to you. What the hell do you say to a white man?'

Only five days later, during the evening when her mother is out at work, Adele answers a rapping on the doorway of her home and is shocked to see the soldier they call the Okie again. He carries a box. Down the street, a small group of astonished neighbours crane their necks but keep to a respectful distance. The soldier smiles.

'Remember me?' he says.

She stares and doesn't reply. Both seem unsure of what to do next, but he lightly taps the box and leaves it with her. She watches him walk down the muddy street and she hears the sound of a jeep starting, though she can't see the vehicle. She notices the neighbours staring, and she pulls the canvas sheet over the door and sits on her bed to see what he has given her.

Treasures from afar. Five more dollars tightly rolled and secured with a muddy elastic band. A package of chewing gum. A thin bar of milk chocolate. A postcard from some part of America showing deep green pines and a lake that looks to any sensible eyes like a sea. Lake Superior, the postcard says. There are also three pictures she recognizes instantly: Gary Cooper, Humphrey Bogart, Marlene Dietrich. Most startling of all, an apple. It's wrinkled and bruised, but an apple nevertheless. Adele stares at the fruit for close to an hour, touching the wrinkles, smelling its skin, even carefully licking the moist bruises. Then, when she can't wait any longer, she cuts it in eighths and eats it down to the core. It is chalky and turned, she later realizes, but she understands it then as the most precious fruit in the world. A promise that something else is possible.

She is crushing the bitter seeds between her teeth when she hears the sounds of her mother approaching. She hears the occasional clop of her shoes on stone, but also the voice of a neighbour.

'We seeing it all now,' he says. 'You training her good, yes, you old whore? You teaching her all you tricks with the soldiers....'

Adele's mother bursts through the canvas door and sees the neat arrangements of gifts on the floor. She asks where they came from and without waiting for a reply she turns upon Adele, pinching her arm tightly and shaking her violently. You are never to talk to them, her mother screams, her eyes wide and awful. You are never, ever, to talk with those people or accept anything they offer you.

'Why?' yells Adele.

'Because I am your mother! Because I tell you so.'

The shaking and pinching grows worse, and Adele fights to free herself. Their struggle becomes so wild that together they tip over the pot that had been sitting on the table for breakfast. The thin porridge spills out upon the floor and Adele's mother immediately kneels to shovel back in what she can. Look what you've done, she hisses. Look what you've done to us. Her horrid chiffon gown rides up her thighs, and Adele notices her torn underwear and the evil wink of her private parts wired with hair. Adele understands it then. This is what her mother wants for them. To eat rubbish off the floor, to crawl about like animals. To suffer even worse than animals.

'You disgusting,' she tells her. 'You a whore.'

'Don't you dare speak to me like that,' her mother answers. 'I is your mother and you don't never speak to me like that.'

'You not my mother. You *horror*. All *horror!*'

Saying this, Adele feels something scorching wash over her,

staggering in its power. But something else too, a chill that begins in her stomach and rises upward. Her mother has stopped shoveling the wasted food from the floor but she is still kneeling, her face down and her shoulders moving as if sobbing. Then, an unexpected sound rises from her. It begins low before rising in volume and pitch until her mother screams it out like laughter. A sound that chases Adele as she flees the house and runs through the streets of Carenage. Then farther still, outside the village, along a path so old that none could remember its origins....

'An out-of-the-way path, she ankles painted cool by the wet grasses. A mango knotting the sky with its branches. It fallen fruit upon the ground. The slick and blackened peels. The drone of drunken insects....'

'Mother...?'

'... a brilliance passing overhead and a silence like glass. I see it then, the creature. It using water in a rusted oil drum as mirror. It putting on she skin, syrup sounds and soft elastic snaps. Gloving on she fingers when it roll she eyes....'

'Mother! How can I tell the story if you don't listen to me?'

She snapped back to the room. She wrinkled her nose at the smell of burned cotton. She quickly put the iron back on the stand.

'You said you going, boy?' she asked casually, distracted by the wedge-shape burn on the shirt. 'Where you going?'

'Where are you going?' the Okie asks. The war was drawing to a close and the security regulations had been relaxed. Still, a coloured girl getting through the base's checkpoint was unusual. The Okie had been polishing his boots in front of his tent when he looked up and called over to the girl who had been leaning against one of the tent-poles across the road, her hands curled under her chin, an unreadable expression on her face. She lifted her head and walked over. Stared for a while at the sight of a white man polishing his own boots. Around her, other soldiers had started to cluster.

'Looks like you've made a friend,' says one, smiling.

'Maybe more than a friend,' says another, laughing.

'Where's your mother?' the Okie asks, ignoring the others.

'I run away,' Adele says, but nothing more.

The Okie asks the others to shut up, but they don't listen. He checks his shirt pocket, shakes out a cigarette and lights it. He blows a plume and hands the girl the lighter once again. She just holds it in her hand, looking up at the faces around her. The whirl of attention. Who is she to have such attention?

'What is she? Five, Okie? Shouldn't you wait until ten?'

'I told you to shut up.'

And then Adele notices it. Her mother's chiffon gown, the image that she had fled since dawn. It has cornered her here. A garment without a body, animated through terrible magics. The jerked and slouching movements as if borne on damaged feet. The emptiness where a head and face should be.

'What's bloody wrong with the guards, today,' shouts a soldier. 'Who the hell is that?'

'Nobody,' answers another. 'The girl's mother. Some whore from Carenage.'

The dress spots Adele and flies toward her as if borne upon storm-winds. A hand appears from the sleeve, and it holds her with a grip that no human could ever match. Adele is dragged like a doll toward the gates of the base, back toward the village and the life that awaits her there, and all about is laughter at this spectacle. Finally, the pulling stops. The dress wheels to face the soldiers, and a voice comes forth like a mother's. It shouts and lays accusations against all those milling about to take in the sport. It calls men by name and shames them and charges them with stupidity and cruelty. It shouts out their unfaithfulness, the helplessness of their bodies, the lies of their manhood. There is a shift in the laughter around her, an uneasiness growing into malice.

'You lies,' she screams. 'You lives of comforting lies....'

A smash of oil and filth in Adele's nostrils. She gasps and staggers with the violence of the attack, and turns just quickly enough to see a soldier moving away with the empty wash bucket. Giggling like an idiot. The water filled with oil and tar and solvents entirely soaks her mother, the intended target, but some of it has splashed upon Adele too, clogging her nose and soaking the back of her neck, her head. It stinks so much she retches. Gasoline vapours. It will never come out, Adele knows instantly. They will forever stink of something shat from the bowels of the earth and cooked in hell. They will never be clean again.

There is a deeper wave of laughter from the soldiers now, and the voice like her mother's dwindles to hoarse sputterings. The grip upon Adele's arm becomes beyond tight, utterly unconscious in the hurt that it creates, and Adele then realizes the great danger she is in, and the need to get away, somehow, from this creature and the entertained eyes around them. She is thinking something like this, or perhaps not thinking at all, when in a miraculous achievement of agility and determination, she flicks the lighter and with a flame that wavers on the verge of dying, holds it to the loose corner of the white sleeve.

There is no poof as when a Hollywood actress gets her picture taken. No explosion or bloom of fire as when something eventful happens in a wartime movie. There is only a thin creeping of a flame in the light of noon, and inside this, visible now for the first time to Adele's eyes, a human form. The woman looks at her belly and arms, watching a miraculous aura grow upon her, smelling the work of something like a hot-comb. She senses more now, and begins to beat at her body, fanning the flames and transferring them about herself. Adele herself feels a pain assaulting her, a sheet of pain on her back and shoulders. A hat of orange light. A halo. She sees her mother in a dress of fire, and she turns toward her, turns to help and undo it all, her mother's arms outstretched too, but she trips and falls heavily against a loose pile of cinder blocks. A numbness and slipperiness at her chin. An inability to open her eyes.

'Jeez,' she hears a voice repeat.

'It's not that bad,' says another. 'It's OK. It doesn't look that bad....'

'Jeez. Oh, jeez....'

'It happened so ... there was nothing we ... the girl ... what was she...? What's wrong with these people...?'

'BUT IT DIDN'T end there, Mother. I also know it didn't end there. You were taken in. You were gathered by people from Carenage who had heard and wanted to help. You were brought back, the two of you, to your home in the village. You were healed with cobwebs....'

'Cobwebs?' she asked.

'The old woman,' I continued. 'She drew them down from the

corners of your house. She laid them upon you like a spell. She gave something to your mother too. Something wet and pithy for the worst of burns. A plant whose name we've both forgotten. Can you remember it now, Mother? Can you tell me this last thing? Today, before I go?'

She was smiling at me, and I caught it. I caught her reading me all the way through. The person I'd become, despite all of her efforts. A boy so melancholy, melancholy despite the luxuries that she'd worked so hard for him to enjoy. A boy moping for lost things, for hurts never his own....

'Mother?'

'Yes, child?'

'Did you really see a soucouyant?'

'Oh dear,' she said, still smiling. 'Whatever you think you want with some old nigger-story?'

I WANTED TO IMAGINE her growing, not diminishing. I wanted to portray her awakening to something that we wouldn't have guessed at otherwise. The freedom of meaning, the wild magic of existence. Geographies slipping into each other. Constellations wheeling above and seasons bleeding into each other so that some wintry neighbourhood can become tropical in an instant. And here she is again taking off her gloves to feel the heat of ice. A dark hand of a man appearing in hers and now she's looking down but cannot see her feet because of her eight-month swollen belly. And again her breasts are leaking milk through her blouse, and a boy with eyes like a mother long ago is sitting in a high chair, another boy tugging at her pants. They would have names, of course. She would have given them names, but what if she didn't? What if they could live in ways beyond such petty details, alive to the teeming…?

'Please listen to me, Mother. Please believe me. I didn't want to sadden you or betray the spell. I didn't want to tell a story like this. I just wanted you to realize that I knew. That I was always close enough to know. That I was your son, and I could hear and understand and take away….'

A cavernous rhythm like the sea. A window looking out upon endless waters. Could she even dream of living anywhere else? This churning spill, this salt-washed power? Why wasn't she smelling the salt anymore…?

She was brought back on that day of my departure by crying. She saw me there, her youngest son. Seventeen at the time and crying.

'You crying?' she asked. 'Why you crying, child of mine, child of this beautiful land?'

'I don't know, Mother. I don't understand anything.'

'You crying and you don't know or understand? Come now, child. Who people children do such silly, silly things?'

'I WAS YOUNG, Meera. I was maybe only four or five. I was standing in shallow water, and I was blessed. I was too scared to go under, and so my grandmother cradled the water over my head. I licked the salt from my lips and everyone laughed. This was a beach near Mother's birthplace. A seaside village named Carenage.'

This is a house on the weathered edge of the Scarborough Bluffs. We're in the sitting room, Meera and I, though there's little, really, to sit on. Just the sturdiest of the boxes, as well as my own packed suitcase. The walls of the room show off-white squares where paintings and photographs once hung. The windows have no curtains and the noon light is white and brittle. It's a rainy day in December, the year's parting joke.

'I know,' says Meera. 'It was an old gesture. Older than anything like religion or history. Your mother told me this many times. She never forgot.'

'But I don't remember it. Not even a little bit. I remember something else from that trip, though. A walk along a shore of hot rocks and trash. My grandmother stumbling and reaching, without thinking, for Mother's hand. Each reaching for the other and then holding hands the rest of the way. I remember being awed by this. It was all so incredibly ordinary. They were just a mother and daughter.'

A passing train and afterward the sounds of the lake. The splash of a rogue wave upon a rock. The single cry of a bird. We're leaving when Meera touches my face.

'Eyestache,' she says.

ACKNOWLEDGMENTS

Sophie McCall, first and foremost, for your love, guidance, and faith during the years it took me to write this book. Anne Stone and Lise Winer for your enormously generous feedback on the last two drafts. Wayde Compton, George Ilsley, Larissa Lai, and Ashok Mathur for your advocacy and companionship. Susan Brook, Kate Cassaday, Jef Clarke, Harvey DeRoo, Lara Hinchberger, Anne-Marie Lee-Loy, and Leslie Sanders for reading earlier drafts of this book, and for your invaluable advice and support. Sepideh Anvar, Laura Arseneau, Oana Avasilichioaei, Brett Grubisic, Daphne Marlatt, and Michael V. Smith for your helpful thoughts on individual chapters and sections. Michael Barnholden, Daniel Coleman, Steve Collis, Andrea Curtis, Jeff Derksen, Peter Dickinson, Kristin Zetta Elliot, Anjula Gogia, Hiromi Goto, Smaro Kamboureli, Bronwen Low, Glen Lowry, Roy Miki, Roxanne Panchasi, Joanne Saul, Priscila Uppal, Karina Vernon, and especially Rinaldo Walcott for your interest, and for your courage when mine fell away. Krystyne Griffin, Ann McCall, Kenneth Ramchand, and K.D. Srivastava for your hospitality. Leith Davis and Carole Gerson for your advice on "The Scarborough Settler's Lament," Elizabeth Kelsen for your advice on dementia, Anand Pandian for your advice on Tamil lullabies, and Lise Winer (once again) for your copious and expert guidance on Trinidadian language and culture. Cindy Mochizuki for your smart drawings and sympathetic script. Robert Ballantyne, Janice Beley, Bethanne Grabham, Shyla Seller, and especially Brian Lam for treating a new author with such patience and honour, and for your heroic work, in general, through Arsenal Pulp Press. Alistair MacLeod for your time and wisdom. Dionne Brand for your support and for your advice about the vocation. Austin Clarke for believing in me and for inspiring a whole new generation. My brother for asking and caring. My parents for so much love, and for anything at all that's good in me and in this book.